HOTEL HOSTESS

Faith Baldwin

Thorndike Press • Chivers Press
Waterville, Maine USA   Bath, England

This Large Print edition is published by Thorndike Press, USA and by Chivers Press, England.

Published in 2002 in the U.S. by arrangement with Harold Ober Associates, Inc.

Published in 2002 in the U.K. by arrangement with the author's estate.

U.S. Hardcover 0-7862-4082-2 (Candlelight Series)
U.K. Hardcover 0-7540-4965-5 (Chivers Large Print)
U.K. Softcover 0-7540-4966-3 (Camden Large Print)

The text of this Large Print edition is unabridged.
Other aspects of the book may vary from the original edition.

Cover design by Thorndike Press Staff.

Set in 16 pt. Plantin by Minnie B. Raven.

Printed in the United States on permanent paper.

British Library Cataloguing-in-Publication Data available

Library of Congress Cataloging-in-Publication Data

Baldwin, Faith, 1893–
    Hotel hostess / by Faith Baldwin.
        p.   cm.
    ISBN 0-7862-4082-2 (lg. print : hc : alk. paper)
    1. Hotels — Employees — Fiction.   2. Large type books.
  I. Title.
  PS3505.U97 H68 2002
    813′.52—dc21
                                                    2002019935

To

GRACE PERKINS and FULTON OURSLER

in friendship and admiration

CAST OF CHARACTERS

JUDITH GILLMORE — the beautiful hotel hostess who knew how to guard a secret.

DR. BILL MARTIN — was skillful but poor.

BERT WALLACE — a wealthy playboy who was unscrupulous with beautiful women.

ALEX CORBIN — owned the hotel. He was like a father to Judith.

BETTY CORBIN — a young enchantress, was crazy about Bill Martin.

SAKS LEWIS — orchestra leader, was wild about Betty.

CANDACE HOWLAND — made a career of manhunting.

GEORGE ELLERTON — once bought off Candace.

AUNT HETTY — just pretended she took no interest in Bill.

CHAPTER I

Miss Manhattan had scrubbed her face and put on her best frock, for spring, her seasonal guest, had come to town. The steel and stone towers aspired to a cleaner blue sky and the warm May sunshine was like a celestial smile. The parks were green, the shrubs had blossomed, the hotel window boxes were gay with flowers. Tulips marched in pink and white rows around the Plaza fountain and walking along Fifth Avenue you saw more pretty girls than you had ever seen in all your life.

One of the prettiest was riding uptown on the top of an open bus. Her name was Judith Gillmore and, as she was a natural redhead with black eyes and a spectacular figure, more than one gentleman occupying space nearby stole appreciative glances at her, moved by the influence of the superbly silly season and the evidence of his own eyes. But Judith was, or appeared to be, oblivious of silent admiration, clearing of throats and straightening of neckties. She was engaged in doing something which no pretty girl in her senses should be doing on a bright May morning. She was indulging in mathematics. She had a notebook and a little pencil and she was methodically setting down figures and adding them up. The sum total did not seem to please her. She drew her fine dark brows together and tapped a small narrow foot with impatience.

The bus slowed to a stop and a girl walking along the Avenue glanced up for no particular reason. But seeing Judith, she stopped in her tracks and shouted. She had a clear and carrying voice.

"Judy! Judy Gillmore!"

Judith jumped and looked down. Then she waved and made frantic gestures.

"Polly!" she called.

"Get off!" yelled Polly with determination.

"Get on!" suggested Judith.

By this time the passengers were much amused, and the bus had started forward slowly.

Polly Andrews was running along beside it, to the disgust of irate taxi drivers.

"Got a lunch date?" she howled, and every man on top of the bus pricked up his ears.

"No," shrieked Judith.

"Then get off at the next corner and

wait," suggested Polly, screaming.

Laughing, flushing a little, Judith pressed the signal button and rose to make her way to the stairs. When the corner was reached and the amused conductor had helped her off, she crossed to the curb and stood there waiting. In a few minutes Polly joined her and they fell into each other's arms with the exuberance of two old friends who have not seen each other for a long time.

"Well, I'll be a so-and-so," said Polly affectionately, "you look like the Federal debt! But more than a billion, my dear, more than a billion. Let's go somewhere and eat like anything and talk like mad. Am I glad to see you, or am I?"

Judith said, smiling:

"You're looking very fit yourself. I'd love to have lunch with you, Polly, if you're sure —"

"Of course I'm sure," said Polly.

"I have to catch a train," Judith told her, "but not until late afternoon."

"Then come along," said Polly, "and make it snappy. I'm dying to hear all about you. Do you realize that we haven't seen each other for four years? Since, in fact, we modestly received the plaudits of the throng upon graduating from dear Miss

Manners, back in the old days."

"Is it only four years?" asked Judith, with a sort of mild wonder.

A little later they were seated at a small, secluded table in a crowded, cheerful restaurant. Polly had suggested, offhand, a half dozen smart and colorful places, the sort of places in which girls of her particular social and financial standing nod carelessly to headwaiters and say, "You've my table, George?" But Judith had other ideas. "This is Dutch," she'd said firmly, "and I can't afford to pay for swank."

"You were always so darned strong-minded!" mourned Polly.

When they had ordered they looked at each other, drew a deep breath and smiled, a little self-consciously. It isn't easy to pick up the threads after four years, no matter how well you'd once known someone. And their lives which, at Miss Manners, had seemed so similar had since diverged, very widely.

Polly spoke first.

"Well," she said. "Look! Can you bear it?"

She thrust out her hand, from which the glove had been drawn. Obediently Judith looked at the big diamond. She said sincerely:

"Felicitations. I hope he knows how lucky he is. And who *is* he, by the way?"

"First name Clarence," admitted Polly, sighing. "Isn't it too too something-or-other? I call him Butch. Last name Worthington. Princeton, thirty-three. He's in his father's business. They make something hideously essential to the motor industry. Gadgets of sorts. Don't ask me what they are. We're being married next month, and taking a world cruise. We'll live in New York, entertain charmingly, get ourselves in the better columns and have three babies before, well, 'forty-two," she ended calmly.

Judith laughed. "You haven't changed, Polly," she said; "you always swore you were going to marry a Princeton man, have an apartment on Park Avenue and a flock of youngsters. I don't know your Clarence, do I?"

"Butch to you," corrected Polly, shuddering. She was a small, very curved blonde with gay blue eyes. "I don't think so. I didn't meet him myself until the summer after we graduated . . . we were on the same boat going to Europe, his father gave him the trip as a graduation present."

"Have you been all that time making up your mind?" asked Judith incredulously.

"I wasn't in love with him, then," said Polly. "There was an Englishman" — she shrugged, and then went on dreamily — "and a Frenchman. And after that the most divine Italian. And then . . . Oh, well," she concluded, laughing, "Butch was very persistent. You know. Quite fatal. The strong, silent kind. So, a little while ago I decided there wasn't any use fighting."

"Happy?"

Polly nodded, sobered for a moment. Then she said, "But you haven't told me anything about yourself. You stopped writing. A year or so ago I wrote you again, to Philadelphia, but the letter was returned, address unknown. And I asked dozens of people . . . and no one knew anything."

Judith's clear skin, fine textured, satin smooth, was a little paler than usual. She said,

"I had the letter you wrote me when Father died, Polly, and I answered it."

"Yes," said Polly, "I sent that to the address I saw in the papers. But afterward, well, I didn't know what to say, Judy. We hadn't seen each other for some time and oh —" She broke off helplessly.

"There wasn't anything you could say," said Judith evenly. "When I left Miss Manners and went back to Philadelphia I took

14

over the running of the house and all that. Mother had been an invalid ever since I was a little girl, you remember?" Polly nodded, and Judith went on, "I'd always had to decide things for myself, you know. Mother couldn't and Father — You met him, Polly, at school and again when you came to visit us that Easter vacation. He was completely the scholar, a dreamer, oblivious to almost everything but his hobbies: early colonial history, old glass, clipper ship prints and books. He expected me to fend for myself, and I'd always managed. I had a big allowance, and Aunt Emily was very helpful; in many ways she took Mother's place. Thanks to her I learned how to handle money, how to run our house, how to dress and all that. Then —" she faltered for a moment, even after all these years, even to someone who knew it was hard to say — "then, Father killed himself."

Polly's eyes were grave, her small face alive with sympathy. She said, low, "Poor old Judy."

"Yes," said Judith gravely. "He — he couldn't take it, Polly. He'd been so engrossed all these years in a world of his own. I sometimes think it was because of Mother. She wasn't at all well almost from the time he married her — and then I was born, and her health was wretched. She couldn't give him the companionship, the partnership a man of his age had a right to expect. But he loved her so much — there was never a question of anyone else for him. So he built a protective shell about himself, and found other interests. He went out very little. He spent most of his time in his library, or with her, reading to her, talking. Summers he had the place in the mountains, and loved it . . . and went in for gardening too, you know. We had the loveliest gardens."

Polly asked as Judith paused, remembering:

"But the money — I mean the man who took it?"

Judith started a little. She had been far away trying to link the possible future with the completed past. She said:

"It was all in the papers. Father inherited his money, you know. And turned it over to a friend to handle. Well, he handed it all right up until two years ago. Then he speculated. He'd gambled with his own money and lost and so he used Father's to try to retrieve his losses. And finally there was nothing left but debts."

"After — after your father died," asked

Polly, "what happened then?"

"There was eventually a small, a very small, income for my mother," said Judith, "after the country place was sold, and the Philadelphia house. Aunt Emily had moved to Chicago, to be near her daughter, my Cousin Evelyn, who'd married out there. She had a pleasant apartment, and her circumstances were moderately good. So, Mother and I went to live with her. It seemed the best thing to do at the time and Mother is happy there, as happy as she'll ever be. She adores Aunt Emily. She's well enough to be up most of the day, to sew a little, to go out for a short drive in good weather. She doesn't need trained care. And Aunt Emily has a couple who have been with her for years: Martha, the woman, is marvelous, a good practical nurse as well as a superb cook. Mother's looked after all right."

"But you," said Polly, "what in the world are you doing? With your looks," she said frankly, "I would have expected that you'd be married long ago."

"I haven't met a great many men at Aunt Emily's," said Judith frankly. "And the ones I knew . . . well, they sort of dropped out of sight. Except for one or two," she admitted. "You remember Tom Carter, don't you? Well, he'd come out to Chicago occasionally."

"He has stacks of money," said Polly, "I remember him perfectly."

"Money or no money," said Judith, shrugging, "Barkis wasn't willing . . . the feminine Barkis in this case."

"I see. And other men?"

"Most of them can't afford to marry a poor girl in this day and age," said Judith, "or, if she's poor she'd better have a job. I hadn't any. I tried, of course. But I wasn't trained for anything. I had a tiny income — you could put it in your eye and not feel it — from an insurance policy which Father took out for me once. At that time he didn't think there was any need for insurance but he had no sales resistance and a nice salesman got to him. I was to have the income on his death, until the policy matured. The income was very small but at least I felt I could buy my own stockings and save up for a dress now and then, and not cut in on the little Mother had or burden Aunt Emily. Then a little while ago the policy matured and I had the choice of continuing the income or taking the principal."

"Which did you do?" asked Polly.

"I took the principal," said Judith, "because I intend to gamble with it."

"For heaven's sake!" said Polly, appalled. "What do you mean, gamble?"

"Well, it's this way. I could take a business course and then look for a job. It's a question whether or not I'd get it. There are so many girls just out of business school looking for jobs. Many of them have people whom they must support. I haven't any talents. I can't act, I can't sing, I can't dance —"

"You dance beautifully!"

"Ballroom stuff," said Judith, "but not professional. Well, I thought it over and talked about it to Aunt Emily. She has an adventurous turn of mind, and finally she agreed with me. The business course seemed just as much of a gamble as anything else, these days. So I blew in most of my fortune on an adequate year's wardrobe. I still had good furs and a little jewelry and I came to New York, and took a room at the Y and thought I'd make a stab at modeling or something."

"And?" questioned Polly, breathlessly, refilling their coffee cups.

"And I lost," said Judith somberly. "Models are a dime a dozen. You have to go to school too and learn to walk and all that. I did get a chance to see how I'd do

19

for commercial photography. But I don't photograph well. My nose is too short or something. Anyway, that's that."

Polly was busy thinking. You could almost hear her brain ticking.

She said, after a moment:

"Look here. I know gobs of people . . . so do Father and Mother and Butch. Between us we'll get you something. And there's scads of room. You come live with us till the wedding. As far as that goes, you can go right on living with us . . . with Mother and Father I mean. Mother's all of a dither because I'm getting married, she'll be lonely as the dickens. She'd adore to have you — she always liked you a lot, Judy. There's a room for you, and you could help her with her letters and things."

She paused hopefully. Judith's eyes were full of tears.

"You're a darling," she said softly, "but I couldn't do it. I can't impose on my friends, my dear."

"It wouldn't be imposing. Oh, Judy," wailed Polly, "what in the world are you going to do?"

"Well," said Judith, "I've one last shot in the locker. Up in Hillhigh, where we had our summer place, there's an all-year-round hotel, the Rivermount. It was built about fifteen years ago and Father helped to back it and he and the manager, Alex Corbin, were good friends. The hotel never paid dividends but that didn't matter to Father; he thought Hillhigh was the loveliest spot in the world and he wanted to see a lot of people enjoy it. Not that they brought anything to him; as a matter of fact, he would rather have been there quite by himself. But he wasn't selfish . . . Not even when — when he killed himself," she said slowly, "because he remembered those little insurance policies, one for Mother, one for me . . . he was thinking of us then. . . . Well, Mr. Corbin writes Mother now and then. And I heard from a friend who'd been to Hillhigh that they let their hostess go the middle of last month. And so I'm on my way up there to apply for the job, if it still exists."

"Hotel hostess?" cried Polly, amazed.

"Exactly. A lot of them — whatever they call themselves, social directors or hotel hostesses — are pests," said Judith firmly. "I've stayed in enough hotels to know. I wouldn't be a pest. And I know how to run a house and meet people. And I can do all the things social directors or hotel hostesses are supposed to do: play contract, ride, swim, drive a car, ski, skate, dance. I wouldn't get much salary but I'd have a room and board, all year round. I have the clothes for it — for a year anyway. So I'm going to take a shot at it."

"But," said Polly, "you're so young!"

"That's the drawback," admitted Judith. "Most of the hostesses are older, some are middle-aged. The young ones are widows as a rule, or divorcees. Well, the least I can do is try. Wish me luck."

"I do. Oh," said Polly earnestly, "you make me tired, Judy. If — if you wouldn't go on being so damned proud. This Dutch business for instance." She looked with distaste at the check which the waitress had brought. "Why can't you let me . . . ?"

"I can't," said Judith, "it's too easy. I've been afraid of it, you see . . . accepting lunches, dinners, weekend invitations, house parties. I could, you know. I could hunt up the old gang here in New York and at home. Lots of them are married now and like to have an extra girl around to fill in. I could spend most of my time visiting. Ashamed because I couldn't tip much, playing contract for more than I could afford if I lost, or letting my partner carry me. You know. I might get to the point where I'd let my partner pay the losses but halve the winnings. I've seen women do that. And all the time I'd be looking for some really eligible man, ready to marry him if I could get him, whether or not I loved him. And after a while I'd be thirty and I'd have a profession, all right. Professional guest and filler-in. Haven't you met them? After the first few years, during which they use people, people start to use them. They are the ones who chaperon the children to parties, who go into town and shop for their hostess, who entertain the drunken elderly gentlemen essential to the host's business but revolting to all his regular women guests. I simply can't let that happen, Polly, so I'm not taking anything. Not even a lunch from you, darling."

"You're crazy," said Polly hopelessly. "I could kill you. But I think you're swell."

"You're pretty nice yourself," said Judith.

Polly went to Grand Central with her and waited there until traintime. Judith's bags had already been checked at the station. She said, reclaiming them, "They've been very nice to me at the Y. They're holding my trunk and other things and when I send them the word they'll express them to Hillhigh, I hope. Otherwise —"

23

"Otherwise what?" demanded Polly.

"Otherwise I return to New York and move out, and back to Chicago, with a flock of good-looking clothes and no place to go. And look for a job there again, without much chance of success. Eventually I suppose I can sell the jewelry and my sables for what they'll bring, and take the business course after all. And you know, Polly, I'll never make that grade because, if you remember me at Miss Manners, I can't spell!"

When the train was made up, she and Polly went to the gates. "You'll write me," Polly said, "and you'll come to the wedding?"

"I'll write but I can't come," said Judith. "If I have a job I can't, and if I haven't I can't either. But if I land the job, Polly, you and your Butch will just have to come to Hillhigh and do me proud. One asset of a successful hostess and social director is to be able to attract the right people. And you, my dear, are the right people if ever I saw any."

"We'll come," Polly promised, "after we get back from Europe, and we'll take the royal suite and insist upon your personal attendance. Good luck, Judy. Step, the gentleman standing outside the train looks restless."

She watched Judith hurry through the gates, carrying her own small bags to the disgust of the redcaps who had viewed her smart suit, tiny tricky hat and excellent sables with confidence. She saw her get aboard and then she turned away. She had to telephone an irate young man and explain why she hadn't lunched with him. Not that it had been a set date. Just, "If you aren't busy, darling, meet me at the Colony." But Butch wouldn't have waited more than twenty minutes. Which was why she hadn't telephoned him from the restaurant. And he'd scold her like anything when she finally reached him. But she didn't care. She liked it.

Walking toward the telephone booth she thought of herself as the luckiest girl in the world, health, a light heart, all the money she'd ever need — and Butch . . . to love her, scold her, quarrel with her, kiss her . . .

Poor Judy, she thought.

CHAPTER II

Judith reached Hillhigh very early on the following morning. She had husbanded her resources and taken a lower berth on a slow local train. There was no diner but she bought fruit, sandwiches and a bottle of Coca-Cola from the train butcher and asked the porter to make up her berth early and so went to bed almost before it was wholly dark. The fact that she would get out at her station around six in the morning did not worry her. She would find something to do between then and nine o'clock.

She was the only one to get off. The crack trains from New York and Boston made the run in about half the time, so visitors to Hillhigh did not have their first glimpse of it on a misty May morning before anyone was up. But Judith had seen Hillhigh at every hour of the day and loved it. She felt rested and ravenously hungry. A weary agent was lounging on the platform and she hailed him.

"Hello, Hank," she said, smiling.

He pushed back his cap and scratched his head. His eyes were very blue. He was tall and lanky and he wore a straggling mustache stained with tobacco juice. He spat and said cordially:

"Judy, ain't it?"

"It is," she admitted, smiling.

"What in time — ?"

"Bad penny always turns up," she said cheerfully. "I'm going up to see Mr. Corbin at Rivermount. Meantime is there any place where I can get some breakfast at this hour? I'm starved."

"You come right along home with me," he said, "my relief's just come. And Prue'll be glad to see you."

"I'd love to," said Judith.

She could accept a ride in Hank's ancient flivver and the hearty breakfast he would share with her. He would not suspect her of any motives and she'd have none. She and Hank were on an equal footing, two human beings, and good friends. She had known him since she first came to Hillhigh, as John Gillmore's little girl, fifteen years ago.

"I ain't seen you," said Hank, clucking at the flivver as if it were a horse, "for a long time."

"About two years," she agreed.

"You ain't changed," he told her. He spat out onto the road. "I was sorry about your

27

dad and all," he said simply.

"Thank you, Hank," she told him gently. "Things haven't changed here either, have they?"

"The mountains never change," he said, "nor the river. People come and go, that's all. Big doings at Rivermount all year round since folks have gone into that skiing business for all they're worth. Beats all how people will suffer for their fun. Broken legs and collarbones, busted ankles and arms. It's wonderful. They come here on the snow trains all dressed up fit to kill, waving them pesky skis around. And half of them go out on stretchers, groaning. But when they mend up they come back again. It's good for business, of course; in the old days we just had weekend parties for sleighing and skating. Now it's most as bad as in summer."

Main Street was just the same. Three blocks of it. The residential side streets had frame houses, set well back, sugar maples, elms, shrubs coming into flower later than in Manhattan. Then country roads, the big estates, Rivermount, the great frame hotel, overlooking the lazy river and the mountains, the altering, eternal mountains, misty green in the sunlight.

She said, "It's the loveliest place in the world."

"You're talking," said Hank.

They were driving down a rutted country road. Hank's house sat back, brown frame, with an ell. It needed paint and the porch sagged. There was a red setter lying in the sun and some chickens cackling about. Hank's wife came out on the porch wiping her hands on her apron.

"You remember Judy," said Hank with finality.

Prudence remembered her, exhibiting no astonishment. It takes a lot to astonish a Yankee. She said, "Come in and set. Breakfast's dished."

Coffee, good cream, oatmeal, a platter of eggs and curly pink ham, biscuits warmed up from last night's supper, wild strawberry jam, the last of last year's gathering.

"Golly!" said Judith with simple greed, and fell to.

Prudence waited on them and finally sat down to a cup of coffee. She'd et, she explained, some time before.

Replete, Judith leaned back in her chair and smiled at her hosts. The sunlight was bright in the kitchen now. The big black cat jumped into her lap and padded softly there before settling down. She said, rubbing his velvet head:

"Tell me all the news."

"Told it," said Hank, lighting his pipe.

"Not much. What about the people who own . . . bought Carcassonne?"

"They call it Bellevue," said Hank. "Dunno as I blame them. The other was a pretty fancy handle. Sounded like something dead to me. They've got a couple of crazy kids, running around in fast cars, always over at the hotel, complaining because they got to go a long ways for a night club or such."

"The Wallaces still live next door?" asked Judith, trying not to remember Carcassonne as she had known it, the beautiful Colonial house, which had been so lovingly remodeled, the tennis courts, the brook which had been dammed to form a pool, the gardens.

"Sure," said Hank, "but they're away. In Europe. All but Bert. He flies up every weekend, in his own plane. Someday he'll break his neck and, as far as I'm concerned, no harm done. His folks expect to be away a year, so he lives at the hotel."

"I never liked him much," said Judith.

"You and me both," said Hank, as Prudence cleared away.

"How's your daughter?" asked Judith after a moment.

"Rose? She's fine. In training, in Boston. Bill Martin says she'll make a fine nurse."

"Bill Martin?"

"Don't you remember him?" asked Hank disapprovingly. "Sure you do. Come from the orphans' home over to Valleytown. Born here, though. Hadn't anyone in the world after his ma and pa died — back in 'seventeen or 'eighteen, wasn't it, Prue? — of the flu. Well, just his Aunt Hetty, here in town. But she wouldn't take him, being a cross-grained old maid that liked his mother and couldn't forgive his father for marrying her. So the home took Bill and kept him till he was eighteen. He used to work odd jobs summers . . . you've seen him around."

"Seems to me I do remember him," said Judith slowly.

"Sure, didn't he do odd jobs for your dad round the gardens?" asked Hank. "He's a fine fellow, Bill. Got himself a scholarship and went to college. Stood ace high in Valleytown when he was at school there. Bert Wallace's father, old Jim, took an interest in him. It was him helped him through college and medical school."

"He's a doctor then?" asked Judith, interested.

"Sure. Had two years in the hospital in Boston. That's how Rose went down there to train, a year ago. She says everyone's crazy about him, especially the women," said Hank, grinning. "But he's back here now . . . working."

"He can't have much practice," said Judith musingly, "except maybe in summer. Now, if he'd settled in Valleytown —"

"I know, but him and Alex Corbin came to some sort of an arrangement. Corbin knew Bill . . . gave him jobs to do after school and summers. Then Betty, Corbin's kid, took sick last fall and was operated on in Boston. Alex saw a lot of Bill Martin and liked him — so does Betty, they tell me."

"Don't gossip," said Prudence severely.

"Well, what's the harm in liking? Anyhow, Alex made a dicker with him. He gives him living quarters and an office in the hotel. Charges him for board, of course, but reasonable. And Bill looks after the hotel people, at the usual fees. He is working up a practice in the town, and goes over to the hospital at Valleytown."

"He doesn't sound overly ambitious," said Judith casually.

"That's where you're wrong. Bill's as ambitious as all get out. But you got to start somewhere. He could've started in Boston; one of the doctors offered to take him as an assistant, but he wants to work in the country. He wants to specialize in kids. There ain't a specialist for kids around here, not even in Valleytown. If he works at Rivermount two-three years he thinks he'll save enough — seeing that he don't have to pay rent — to get started. He's a good boy . . . a little quick on the trigger, perhaps, got a temper. Not that it ever harmed a man none."

Prudence, still clearing away, said:

"Judy's not interested in Bill Martin. I'd like to know what brings you here, Judy."

"I'm looking for a job," said Judy, smiling. "A friend of mine was up here for a weekend not very long ago and said Mr. Corbin had let his hostess go."

"Let her go!" snorted Prudence. "She went like a — a skyrocket. Lots of noise and excitement."

Hank chuckled.

"She come down to the station with forty-'leven bags and blood in her eye," he announced. "Was she mad!"

"What happened?" asked Judy, laughing.

"Did you know her?" asked Prudence cautiously.

Judith shook her head.

"She was one of these blondes," said Prudence, "with baby curls, and little hands and feet. I did some sewing for one of the boarders last summer and this Mrs. Robins — I seen her a lot of times, when I went over — always sat in the biggest chair she could find so her feet would dangle. Wore them open-toed sandals and painted her toes red, like a Comanche Indian. I don't know exactly what happened, but round town they was saying that there was a man there last fall and she went after him hammer and tongs. Spent most of her time playing tennis with him, and golf and walking and all that, and sat at his table. Mr. Corbin didn't like it any too well, and there was a big row. He was there three weeks and then come up weekends for winter sports. She went around telling folks that they were engaged and she had a ring that would knock your eye out. But his wife turned up. Seems she'd been in Europe taking a cure or whatever they call it."

"Rule Number One," said Judith: "Don't neglect the guests for a private hunting."

"You're pretty young," said Prudence doubtfully, "for that sort of job."

"That's what they all say," admitted Judith, sighing. She put the cat off her lap and rose. "Well, I'll get along," she told them, "and thanks a lot for breakfast. I needed it. I wonder —" she hesitated a little — "I wonder if I could leave my bag here? Because if Mr. Corbin won't take me on . . . well, I'll get the first train back to New York."

"Got a round-trip ticket?" asked Hank.

"No," said Judith, "one way."

"Optimistic, ain't you?" he asked, grinning.

"Either that or crazy," she told him, laughing.

He pulled out his watch and glanced at it.

"I'll drive you to Rivermount," he said, "got plenty of time."

Judith shook her head.

"It's too early," she told him, "and I'd like to walk. It's such a grand day. I thought I'd stop and see people . . . you know, look over the fence and holler and see if they remember me."

A little later she had said good-bye temporarily, left her bag and was walking toward the village, through which she must pass before reaching Rivermount. There weren't many people about but those that were looked at her curiously, a slender girl, with a slim waist and broad shoulders, walking as if she liked to walk, wearing casual tweeds and a sable scarf, a tiny hat far back on her red head. Now and then someone paused and looked after her frowning . . . hadn't they seen her before — her hair was an unusual color.

She stopped in the post office and presented a smiling face at the window, and the fat, gray-haired woman who was Hillhigh's postmistress cried, "Why, Judy Gillmore!" and came from behind the official window to talk and exclaim and said inevitably, "I'd have known you anywhere."

She stopped at the drugstore to see old "Doc" Allen, and at the stationery store to see if Steve Baker still ran it, but he did not and the stranger behind the counter eyed her without interest. Beyo'nd the village on the way to Rivermount she saw Mr. Alcot, the pastor of the white-spired church, walking in his front yard examining his fine French lilacs which were just beginning to show color, and stopped to lean across his picket fence and hail him. He was delighted to see her; he took off his glasses, wiped them carefully, put them on again and beamed all over his thin fine face. He had known her since first she came to Hillhigh and to the Sunday school. He had written her at the time of her father's death and she counted him among her good friends. She told him, when he asked her to come in and sit with him under the grapevine in the warm sunlight, why she had come back.

"I see no reason why you shouldn't have the position," the old man said gravely, "you're a level-headed girl, Judith. And if you'd like me to speak a word to Mr. Corbin . . ."

When she left him her heart was lighter and she hurried a little, up the country road to the Rivermount's gates. A song sparrow sang nearby and a flash of blue across her vision was a bluebird. Gravely she took off her little hat and bowed. "Thanks," she said aloud, a pretty red-headed girl talking to herself on the country road.

A small battered car, furiously driven, passed her so close that she jumped back, scrambling to safety. She was furious. She had had an impression of a dark and reckless young man who didn't look where he was going. She yelled after him without dignity: "Why don't you look where you're going?" After all, he must have seen her for a considerable distance. What if she was walking in the middle of the road? . . . he needn't come up on her that fast, she told herself irritably.

She climbed the hill to Rivermount and saw the big hotel, in its lawns and gardens, with the tennis courts on the left and the stables in the distance and the golf links on the other side stretching down almost to the watered blue silk of the river. The place looked rather deserted. Just a few youngsters running about and some elderly people sunning themselves in chairs on the veranda.

Judith climbed the steps, took a deep breath and marched in. A moment later she was sitting with Alex Corbin in his office.

Corbin was a stocky man with a broad, pleasant face. He kept shaking his head and saying, "I can't believe my eyes. Where's your luggage?"

She explained, smiling:

"I haven't come as a guest, Mr. Corbin. But as a potential employee — I hope. The hostess job."

"My dear girl!"

She spoke rapidly, but without nervousness.

"Yes, I know. I'm too young. But need that be such a drawback? You know that from the time I was sixteen I took my mother's place in our house as hostess, except when I was in school. At eighteen, completely. I know how to meet people, Mr. Corbin, how to make them comfortable and at ease. I — I don't mind children, even the sort of children hotels are fated to have — and I like old people." Her black eyes were very grave. "I — I'm sensible enough," she said, smiling, "and I can do all the required things. I'd work hard. I'd efface myself, I mean I wouldn't bounce around bothering people. I've been in a lot of hotels and I know that a social director can make herself very obnoxious. But I could arrange parties and social contacts for the old people and the lonely, I could look after the youngsters. If — if you'd give me a chance. And I don't mind being a fourth at contract!"

He nodded. "I believe you. But it isn't easy. You're on the job from the time you get up until you go to bed, and that's often very late. You haven't much time for dates of your own. You have one afternoon and evening off a week, and something sometimes comes up and you don't get that. And it's all year round, for since the skiing craze hit us we're almost as busy in winter as in summer."

She said, "If you'd try me? You don't get a really big crowd till after the schools close. But there'll be enough people in the hotel from Memorial Day on anyway to —" She broke off, smiled appealingly. "You understand. Try me, won't you? If you think I won't work out, then you can get someone more competent before the crowd starts coming. I need the work, Mr. Corbin, and I want it."

He said slowly, "Well, I don't know —"

They talked back and forth, argued, discussed. At the end of half an hour he smiled at her and leaned back in his big chair.

"All right. You've convinced me that your qualifications far outweigh your youth and inexperience. I'll try you. The salary . . ." He hesitated, named a sum, and looked at her from under heavy brows. "Is that all right?"

"Of course."

"You'll have your room and bath and board," he told her. "Your expenses —"

She said rapidly, "Laundry, tips, clothes. Well, I have the clothes, at least." She smiled brilliantly. "Lots of them. I bought them with the job in mind."

"You were pretty sure," he began, smiling.

"I had to be. Nowadays you must be sure," she said somberly, "for if you once start doubting . . ."

He said, "I'm glad you're coming to us. When can you come?"

"Right away. I left my bag at Hank Parsons'. I'll wire the place I was staying in New York to send on my trunks."

"You remember Betty," he asked, "my daughter? She's graduating from school this June. Just eighteen. It will be nice for her to have you here. She's a wonderful kid," he said, his good face tender, "but a handful. It isn't easy for a man to bring up a daughter, especially a pretty one."

When she left him everything was settled, her heart sang with the spring. There were a hundred things on her mind: the wire to her mother, the wire to the Y.W.C.A., her bag to be collected, and she must stop and see Mr. Alcot. She was happy, wildly happy — and she did not see the dark young man with the small black bag in his hand rush down a corridor and into the almost empty hotel lounge. They collided violently, to the amusement of the desk clerk and of an old lady who was knitting in a great bay window.

The shock rocked Judith on her feet, the black bag hit the floor and opened, spilling bottles and jars and strange-looking implements. The young man swore and bent to retrieve them. Judith gasped, breathless, and the young man demanded angrily:

"Why don't you look where you're going?"

CHAPTER III

"I'm sorry," Judith apologized, automatically, and then as her breath returned and her spirit asserted itself she added, in astonished annoyance, "but I don't see why I *should* be!"

"What's that?" inquired the human projectile, down on his knees engaged in repacking his bag. He looked up, slammed the last object, a stethoscope, into the bag, and rose. "Did I hear you correctly?" he inquired with deceptive calm.

"You certainly did." She was laughing now. Her color was high and her eyes were very black. "I was walking along, minding my own business, an innocent bystander — or bywalker, if you prefer — and harming no one, when you came barging out of the corridor like a bombshell. I think the shoe is on the other foot, Dr. Martin."

She had placed him, of course; an impetuous young gentleman with a black bag. He gaped at her a moment solemnly. He was, she saw, now that matters were restored to a semblance of normality, an attractive person, despite the gape and the beginning of a scowl. Very dark hair, un-usually blue eyes, a brown skin, white teeth a little crooked, a belligerent jaw and a high-bridged nose.

He had the bag in his hand and was glowering down at her. He said, "You have the —"

"Please don't say I have the advantage of you," implored Judith. She straightened her little hat. "I'm Judith Gillmore."

He looked at her, the scowl vanished and a slow smile touched the corners of his mouth. "So you are," he said, as if amazed, "I thought I knew you. I said to myself, 'That hair could only —'" He stopped, looked faintly embarrassed and added calmly, "Well, we're even, then."

"Even?"

"Why not? Once, a good many years ago, I was raking leaves on your lawn and you rode over me on a bicycle," he informed her.

"I never did . . . I . . . oh golly," said Judith, "I do remember."

A lanky little girl with pigtails on a new bicycle, and a big, odd-job boy raking leaves. And Judith flying by, the pigtails streaming, calling, "I'm sorry," and the boy picking himself up out of the leaves, examining a bumped knee and calling down silent maledictions on the departing redhead.

She held out her hand.

"Quits, then, Dr. Martin?"

"Quits, Miss Gillmore."

They walked toward the lounge doors and Bill Martin asked, "Can I take you anywhere? I'm on my way to the village."

"Would you?" asked Judith. "I was going to walk, but now you're here — if you'd let me off at Hank Parsons'?"

"Hank a friend of yours?"

"Indeed he is. I left my bag at his house."

"Coming up to stay here?"

"For good," said Judith firmly, and crossed her fingers.

"For good?"

"I'm the new social director," she explained, "the hotel hostess."

"Well, I'll be a —" He left the sentence unfinished. Now they were going down the steps and the battered car was in evidence.

Judith looked at it and then at him. "And by the way," she said, "talk about not looking where you're going! You nearly ran over me less than an hour ago!"

"Was that you? Why in time do you have to walk in the middle of the road?" he asked severely.

Judith climbed in beside him and sighed.

"I give up," she said sadly, "and I refrain from asking you why you have to drive fifty miles an hour and why you didn't warn me that you were coming."

"I was in a hurry," said Dr. William Martin.

"That," said Judith, "was obvious."

He guided the car down toward the village with a slightly more cautious hand. At that, a corner on two wheels seemed to be routine, and Judith murmured, "Never a dull moment," as they skittered around the first turn.

"A sissy, eh?" demanded Bill, grinning. "Can't take it?"

"Not at all," she said with dignity, "but I would like to survive long enough to try to hold my first job."

He slowed their speed and said gravely:

"I — I heard about your father, Miss Gillmore. I was more than sorry. He was very good to me."

"He was good to everyone," she said, low, and there was a little silence as the car bounced and wheezed and whirred along the roads. The trees were coming into their new fresh green and in the stronger sunlight the mountains were green and violet and deep blue, with that clean-washed look as if not so long ago snow had lain upon them cold and pure and lovely.

He said, after a moment:

"I hope you like your job. It's no cinch. You have to maintain a bedside manner twenty-four hours a day, so to speak."

Judith laughed.

"I think I know what I'm up against," she told him, "but I'm not afraid."

"No, I doubt if you're afraid of anything very much," he said.

"I'd prefer to take that as a compliment," she told him, "so I won't inquire how you meant it. But I *am* afraid — of a lot of things."

"What, for instance?" he asked, interested, and then, as she hesitated, "Come across, doctors are used to confidences."

"But you aren't my doctor," she reminded him.

"I will be," he told her cheerfully. "You're a hotel employee, aren't you?"

"Yes, thank heaven! Well then," she said, sobering, "I'm afraid of failure — and of poverty — and of loneliness — and of illness."

He shook his head. After a moment he said:

"So am I. Do you suppose everyone is?"

"Of course," said Judith.

"Funny thing, your knowing that," he told her, remembering the beauty and peace and charm of Carcassonne and the kid on a bicycle without a care in the world. "I grew up knowing," he added, "every waking moment . . . telling myself, 'You've got to get out of this, you've got to be *somebody*.'"

They were passing a small brown house of nondescript appearance. Dormer windows looked like eyebrows and shades were drawn down like eyelids. There was one lone lilac tree in the neglected front yard and a bent, elderly woman was engaged in coaxing a cat from the high branch of a maple. She had a shawl about her head and shoulders, and wisps of gray hair straggled out from a dour, weatherbeaten face.

Bill honked his horn. "Hi, Aunt Hetty!" he shouted.

The woman turned, and then turned back again, every line of her bent figure expressing disapproval. Bill laughed shortly.

"That," he said, "is my only living relative, my father's sister. She hates me. Or perhaps you'd have guessed without my telling you."

"I remember Miss Hetty Martin," said Judith, feeling absurdly sorry for him; "she

47

had the little sweet shop by the post office, didn't she? And lived in back?"

"That's Aunt Hetty."

"I used to buy all-day suckers there," said Judith, "and once I rescued her cat from a fight with somebody's dog. She gave me a licorice stick. We were quite friendly after that."

"You should have a medal," said Bill gloomily. "She hasn't been friendly with anyone before or since. It's probably her glands," he added, smiling, "but infuriating nevertheless. I always yell at her when I go by because you can't tell — someday she may yell back. Lord knows *what*, I shudder to dwell on it! But once in a blue moon it might be, 'Hello, Bill, come on in and have a cup of tea.'"

"She's a wretch," said Judith severely.

"Oh, I don't know. She was a lot older than my dad and thought he was pure gold. She was jealous of him, and when he married my mother . . ." Bill shrugged. "Not that it matters," he went on, "but when Mother and Father died everyone thought she'd take me. But she wouldn't. She proved to the satisfaction of all concerned that she wasn't the person to have me, that she couldn't, in fact, afford me. My parents had friends, and they had pull.

So the orphanage got me. They were good to me there, I have no kick."

Judith had. She would have liked to shake the old woman. She said, with spirit, "I'm sorry I rescued her darned cat!"

"That's nice of you," said Bill quite soberly. "Well, maybe I wouldn't have been as happy with her as at the Home. Only kids are sensitive. It's a queer feeling not to have anyone of your own, and a queerer feeling to have someone who doesn't want you. But that's all washed up, ancient history."

"She gave up the sweet shop?" asked Judith.

"Yep, too sour for it," said Aunt Hetty's nephew. "Moved into the brown house which she'd rented before and now lives on heaven knows what. Well, here we are at Hank's."

He stopped the car suddenly, and jumped out to help her out. "When are you coming back to the hotel?" he asked.

"I've just to get my bag."

"Okay. Let's pick it up now, and if you don't mind going on a couple of calls with me, I'll drive you back. I made some calls this morning and was whizzing home —"

"I'll say you were whizzing!"

"Skip it — to write up some charts and

things when I got word that I was wanted again. So, step on it, will you? Or shall I call back for you?"

"No, I won't be a minute."

She sped through the yard and into the house and Prudence who had been looking out the window, opened the door.

"Isn't that Bill Martin?"

"In person. He's going to take me back to the hotel. I got the job!" Judith took Prudence in her strong young arms and hugged her soundly. "You'll be seeing a lot of me," she told her. "May I come down on my days off?"

She picked up the bag before Prudence could say more than "For heaven's sake, of course you can!" and was off down the steps. Bill came to meet her and take the bag from her hand.

"Whoops," he advised, "hold your hat, we're off!"

Their first call was at the drugstore and then out of town on rutted country roads to a farmhouse.

Sagging gate and overgrown yard. A spick-and-span barn, big, new and fine, with two silos. A house which needed paint and a carpenter. The gingerbread on the eaves broken and hanging, the porch steps in bad condition, and on the porch a broken rocker, a chair covered with carpeting, a child's roller skates. In the yard some aimless hens and a nondescript dog. Apple trees, the buds pink and tight. A pear tree, white foam.

Judith sat there waiting, smiling a little to herself, thinking of all this day had brought her, when she was startled by a yell.

"Hey," shouted Bill, appearing from the porch, "come in here, will you?"

Astonished but docile, she climbed out of the car, picked her way across the yard, gingerly ascended the steps and confronted him.

"Come in," he said impatiently. "Believe it or not, I've got to pull a tooth! It seems that Doc Peters, the Valleytown dentist, is down with grippe and young Master Stevens's tooth has to come out. His mother can't do anything with him, his father's out plowing, which leaves me high and dry. I'd like to wring his neck. Give me a hand, will you? — it will take two of you to hold him."

"But I can't," began Judith, but Bill had seized her hand and was dragging her across the threshold.

It wasn't the neat New England farmhouse of your dreams. It was anything but tidy and it smelled to heaven of decaying apples, cabbage, mustiness, old wood and smoke. In the kitchen, where chairs jostled the range, tables on three legs collapsed drunkenly against the wall and a large broken-down couch occupied one corner, a small boy was howling dismally. His face was tied up in a rag and one side looked like a chipmunk that has found winter provender. Master Stevens was indulging in an orgy of self-pity and his mother stood by helpless. A thin woman, perhaps thirty years old, she looked fifty. She wasn't very clean. Neither was Master Stevens.

"Come on now," ordered Bill, "open your mouth."

Master Stevens kept it shut and shook his head.

Then he saw Judith.

"Who's that?" he inquired suspiciously, still keeping his mouth shut as much as possible.

"She's a nurse," replied Bill mendaciously, "she's going to help you."

Judith smiled at the swollen and sullen child.

"Listen," she said, and took his hand, which was hot, damp and dirty, "did your mother tell you it wouldn't hurt?"

Fascinated, Master Stevens nodded.

"That was just because she wanted to

make it easy for you," pursued Judith, to Bill's horror and the mother's amazement. "It will hurt. But not as much as it hurts now. And once it's out it won't hurt at all. Only girls make such a fuss about a little pain. Boys don't. Not real boys. You *are* a boy, aren't you?"

"You betcha I'm a boy!" said Master Stevens, annoyed.

"Okay," said Judith cheerfully, "prove it to us. Open up that mouth and we'll believe you."

He opened it, to his own astonishment. Judith seized him strategically, his mother took his hands. After a brief struggle Bill emerged victorious, the tooth a trophy. Master Stevens, bloody and unbowed, howled some more. He was heard to mutter something about a dirty trick.

"Well, I declare," said Mrs. Stevens, wiping her hands on her apron. "That was just fine. What do I owe you, Bill?"

Everyone, decided Judith, called him Bill. She would too.

"What does Dr. Peters charge you?" he inquired.

"Fifty cents."

"Make it a quarter," said Bill. He slapped Master Stevens on the back. "You'll cut a great figure at school tomorrow," he told him, "when you show the other fellows the hole in your face. Too bad it isn't a little more to the front," he said critically, "or you could spit through it like nobody's business!"

Master Stevens was not much appeased by the idea of returning to school. However, he put his hand cautiously to his jaw and decided that he felt better. He grinned at Judith. "I *am* a boy," he said proudly, "ain't I?"

His dirty little face was wreathed in sudden smiles when Bill took the coin which Mrs. Stevens had fished from a worn pocketbook lying on the tin icebox, and dropped it into his hand. "For every tooth a quarter," he said, "but I advise you not to buy candy with it for a day or two."

"Gee!" said Master Stevens, awed. "Thanks, doc."

"Bill, you shouldn't . . ." began Mrs. Stevens, agitated.

He put his arm around her. "Nonsense," he said cheerfully. "This isn't my job anyway. Look here, Nellie, I want you to have him rinse out his mouth often with salt and water." He went on explaining, as Judith looked about her a little heartsick at the disorder and the confusion and concluded presently, "His teeth aren't any too good, are they? Does he get plenty of milk and fresh vegetables?"

A little later when they were in the car, he said soberly:

"Stevens is a good farmer. His cows are in perfect condition, his barns spotless. But his house and his family!" He shrugged. "They don't bother to grow their own table truck, they live out of cans. They sell all the milk. Nellie's been ill ever since the kid was born. She had him here at home under pretty bad conditions and the people who took care of her — Well, it isn't a pretty story, and it's none of my business. But it makes me boil. I've always known Stevens, and Nellie and I are the same age, we went to grade school together. She married at seventeen, lost three kids before she had this one: one was born dead and the other two had diphtheria. All the ignorance and poverty aren't in city slums, but in this case it's ignorance and stubbornness. Because Stevens makes a good living. Every time he has a surplus he buys more cattle."

Judith said slowly:

"I thought all farmhouses were —"

"Like Hank's house? Well, think again. Of course the majority are decent enough, and the men buy their wives the labor saving devices . . . but here and there you'll find a man like Stevens who'll live in dirt up to his neck and let his wife drag herself around half sick and never think about it as long as his barns are the best in the township. By the way, thanks a lot for helping out, you were swell."

"Just applied psychology," said Judith, laughing. "By the way, I didn't enjoy that little scene any more than you did. Or as well. I hate blood!"

"You do? You don't look the swooning type. Well, thanks all over again then. Now I've got to deliver some medicine here and then I'll take you back to the hotel."

As they drove up the road to Rivermount Judith sighed and Bill looked at her curiously.

"What's it all about?" he inquired.

"Nothing. Just that I love Hillhigh and am so glad to be back."

"And now," he told her, "the job begins. You haven't much to work on for a starter. Some kids; a youngster, who's here with her aunt, convalescing from pneumonia — nice kid, I'm looking after her; some old people; and a few of the regulars, all-year-rounders: Mrs. Orson, Mrs. Renwick and old Mr. Smith. weekends will be busier. Not scared, are you?"

"No." She smiled at him as the car came to a stop and he commented, grinning, "Well, we didn't get off to a very auspicious start, did we? But we're old friends now. And if there's anything I can do . . ." He held out his hand. "Bill, meet Judy," he said gravely, "Judy, meet Bill."

She put her hand in his. "Hello, Bill," she began, when there was a shriek from the direction of the veranda and an extremely pretty blond girl came flying down the steps. "Bill," she called, "Bill *darling!*"

CHAPTER IV

"Betty, for Pete's sake! Why aren't you in school?" asked Bill and leaped from the car.

He's forgotten me, thought Judith. Her moment of contentment with life, her sense of high adventure and of a heart-warming friendliness had passed and she got out slowly and went up the steps where Bill was vainly trying to extricate himself from the embrace of Alex Corbin's daughter.

"This," he said to Judith, "is Betty Corbin. Betty, you remember Judith Gillmore?"

"Of course I do. I had the worst crush on you, Miss Gillmore, about four years ago when I was just a kid. You used to come over to the dances with Bert Wallace and a half dozen others and I'd hang around corners and hope you'd smile at me."

Judith said, smiling now:

"That was sweet of you. And I do remember you."

"Dad just told me," the girl cut in, hanging to Bill's arm with one hand and to

Judith's with the other. "I'm thrilled to death. I mean it's too marvelous that you're going to be here with us. What a divine hat!"

"Don't mind her," said Bill, "she just runs on like that. Even under ether. Betty, what in the world are you doing at home?"

"Isn't it silly," she said, making a face at him, her blue eyes crinkled at the corners, "but they've measles at school. So I've been shipped home. The graduating class will go back for a week and graduate after it's all over. I've had 'em, I thought I could stay, but only six out of the seventy girls were immune or something. Anyway, they've turned the school into a hospital and here I am."

"Oh," said Judith, remembering, "my bag."

Bill said, "I'll get it," and ran down to the car.

Betty looked at the older girl with open friendliness.

"It's going to be grand having you here," she said. "I hated the last one — that Mrs. Robins — and the one before. They were too sick making, but this is keen. We'll have such fun. I've asked three of the girls who live in Boston to come up and spend a week or so with me. We'll plan things —

you will, won't you?" she asked anxiously. "Oh, boy," she concluded with enthusiasm, "what a chaperon you'll make!"

Her duties, Judith decided, were beginning with a vengeance.

"And Bill," said Betty, "isn't he marvelous? I'm crazy about him. But *crazy!* My dear, if you could have seen him in the hospital, in his white coat, looking around the door at me and saying —" She broke off as Bill came back with the bag.

"Well," he said, looking from one to the other, "here we are."

Judith had luncheon at the Corbin table with Mr. Corbin and Betty. Bill was nowhere to be seen. The big dining room seemed very empty with but a few of the tables occupied, but Corbin assured her that weekends found them quite full and from Memorial Day on there would be a constant coming and going. Meantime there were some conventions, beginning next week, which would keep them busy.

"Your room all right?" he wanted to know.

"It's fine," she said, "so sunny and big and with that river and mountain view. I've wired for my trunks, and as soon as they come I'll get myself settled. Meantime, there must be things I can do."

There were. After luncheon Corbin presented her to the guests, and showed her the small desk in the lounge that was to be hers. It bore a framed card: SOCIAL DIRECTOR. And back of it was the bulletin board on which it would be her duty to post the typewritten reminders of various activities. Closeted with Corbin in his office during the afternoon she looked through the files of former activities at the hotel. Riding parties, picnic parties, sailing parties, dances, contract, biweekly motion pictures in the ballroom, special activities for the children, golf tournaments, tennis matches, badminton, swimming contests . . .

"Think you can manage?" he asked.

"I'm sure I can. And I've a date this very afternoon," she told him, smiling.

"A date?"

"I'm going driving with Mrs. Renwick. I had a little talk with her after lunch. It appears she doesn't like to drive alone and she's had a little disagreement with Mrs. Orson . . ."

"Mrs. Renwick," explained Corbin, "has three million dollars and no relatives — except a niece whom she loathes. She lives here all year round. She doesn't like Florida or California and she's afraid to go to Europe. We have had her four years. She has a personal maid, a car and a chauffeur, and no friends. My former hostesses were utterly unable to get along with her. Don't let her impose on you, Miss Gillmore."

"Judith, to you."

"Judith then. But everyone calls you Judy."

"You may too," she said, "if you like it better."

"Well, she's terribly exacting," he said, "and of course we want to keep her contented. She has the pleasantest suite in the hotel, and is, I must say, very generous to the staff. But she isn't easy to handle."

"Thanks for the warning," said Judith, smiling. "I'll do my best. Any more helpful hints?"

"Mrs. Orson," said Corbin, "is Mrs. Renwick's best friend. They are at swords' points half the time but depend on each other. Old Mr. Smith, who is also one of our regulars, is a different matter. If you keep him supplied with library books, look after his occasional guests and accept his invitation to dinner at his table now and then, he will be perfectly happy. Another of our regulars — that is, he flies up almost every weekend — is your old friend Bert Wallace."

"Yes," said Judith without enthusiasm, "I had heard that his house was closed."

"He spent a holiday vacation with us at Christmas," said Mr. Corbin, "and will spend some of the summer here, as well as weekends." He paused, looked fixedly at a paper knife and said, as if casually, "His father, as you perhaps know, underwrote our indebtedness here."

Well, thought Judith, that's something of a warning. Not that I need it . . . Bert and I always got along fairly well.

Corbin looked up smiling.

"Betty is most enthusiastic about you. I can't tell you how glad I am that you're going to be here with her. . . . Is there anything further you would like to ask me?"

By Memorial Day Judith had her new job pretty well in hand. She had devoted herself to Mrs. Renwick whenever possible, patched up the trouble between that bewigged and formidable old lady and her fat friend, Mrs. Orson, and had persuaded old Mr. Smith to make a fourth at contract, several evenings, immolating herself on the altar of duty. Mr. Smith had never before permitted himself to be drawn into what he scornfully called the old women's brigade, but he didn't mind with Judith facing him across the table. She had arranged a

63

picnic, with lunch cooked out of doors, for Betty and her school friends, even rounding up three of the visiting weekend young men. She had helped take care of a Mrs. Pendleton, at Rivermount for a short stay and stricken with influenza, until a nurse was available from the Valleytown Hospital, and had made arrangements by telephone for Mrs. Pendleton's daughter to come up from New York and take her home when she was well enough to travel. She had assisted, capably but not without revulsion, when Bill Martin found it necessary to do a neat and minor bit of lancing on one of the floor maids. And she had made her plans for that first big weekend.

Bert Wallace had not flown up, as they had expected, during her first weekend at Rivermount. He came and went much as he pleased, his rooms were reserved for him at all times. Judith was rather glad of his nonappearance. She had known him not only as her next-door neighbor, but in New York and on her frequent visits there. He had been a rather overbearing, if extraordinarily good-looking, young man and she had always held a grudge against him . . . because of Ruth Cummings.

Ruth had visited her during the Gillmores' last summer at Hillhigh and Bert had given her a magnificent rush. Ruth, susceptible and shy, had taken his lightest word for gospel and had managed in a brief month's time to break, or at least fracture, her little heart. Ruth was married now, happily, and living in California, but Judith had never forgotten the last night of her visit. She had sat with her in the big pleasant guest room until the early summer dawn and listened to what she had to say. It hadn't been much, she'd cried so hard.

Vainly Judith had tried to persuade her that she'd forget all about Bert Wallace in another month, but Ruth hadn't believed that — then. She'd been too hurt. Like most women, she'd blamed Bert's sudden loss of interest not on his own character but on that of the other visiting girl who had swept into town on the last week of her visit and taken his attention completely.

"If it hadn't been for her . . ." she wept.

"Listen," Judith recalled herself saying in exasperation, "he isn't worth it, Ruth. Honestly, he isn't."

Nor had he been, she thought.

Memorial Day weekend was a three-day weekend that year. The guests began to pour in on Friday and there was a constant confusion of arrivals. The last of the conventions had gone, although there would be more in June but for this long weekend the visitors were mostly blithe young creatures out for a very good time. The hotel would see that they had it. The stables were ready, the horses polished down to the last hoof. Picnics were planned, and hikes. There were to be two dances, a motion picture, a concert. And for the dances there would be the new orchestra.

"College kids," Mr. Corbin had explained to Judith; "their first real job. They're willing to come from the end of May to after Labor Day. The leader, Lewis, graduated last June and has been kicking around ever since, getting his boys together, playing short engagements. I met him through one of the guests, this winter, in Boston. He was tickled to death to get the job, board and lodging for the summer. He's a nice youngster, a little crazy, and he has a good band. We've found that our young people aren't so apt to drive fast and furiously to the summer roadhouses if we can give them more than the usual or biweekly dances here. So, this season there'll be dinner dancing in the grill every night in addition to the Wednesday and Saturday night dances in the ballroom."

Saks Lewis and his boys came up early, to be on tap. Judith saw a lean and smiling young man, with what is known as personality plus, a pleasant tenor voice, and a curl in his dark hair. His boys were young, enthusiastic, delighted at an opportunity to have their cakes and coffee provided for a whole season. They were housed in one of the small hotel cottages and professed themselves perfectly content.

On Friday Bert Wallace flew up from New York. The hotel maintained a private landing field and small hangar for private planes and Bert flew in, circled low over the buildings, and made an excellent three-point landing on the field.

He had wired when he was to be expected and one of the garage attendants drove the short distance in the small car, which Bert kept at Rivermount, to pick up him and his luggage.

Judith was at her desk when he came in, and very busy. Mrs. Renwick had decided to give a small dinner party and had left the arrangements to Judith, flowers, place cards, seating. She must also see to it that there were flowers in the room of each incoming guest, together with a personal note from her as social director. There were a hundred and one things to attend to and she was too new at her job, and too anxious, to take them in her stride. She had asked Mr. Corbin if she could not inaugurate the pleasant custom of afternoon tea in the lounge for all the guests who happened to be about at the time. It would serve to get them together, the necessary introductions could be made more pleasantly and she would preside. There were always lonely people, especially elderly people. There were always girls and their parents. You had to be careful, she thought, frowning at her list, but heaven helping she would try not to make mistakes.

Someone loomed up at her desk, a shadow between herself and the sun. Someone said, "I wouldn't believe it if I didn't see it with my own eyes!"

It was Bert Wallace, big, tanned, beaming. Judith looked up and smiled at him, giving him her hand.

"Hello, Bert," she said, "we've been expecting you."

He squinted down at the card on the desk.

"Is this a gag?" he demanded.

"No, of course not. It's a job," she said evenly.

She was looking, he thought, prettier than he had remembered her. She wore a cool linen frock with a little jacket and her hair was in loose burnished curls about her temples.

"Trying to see how the other half lives?"

"Don't be silly," she said a little shortly. "This isn't a pastime with me, Bert, it's a job."

Lots of the girls he knew worked. Some for amusement, some because their allowances had been cut recently, some because they were natural exhibitionists. And some because they really had to work. He knew dozens of them. But he kept the two kinds apart. Judith fell into neither category. She was a girl he had always known, a girl he'd rather admired but who had never given him a tumble, and now she was working because she needed the money. She was alone, living in a hotel that was virtually his father's, and the situation might be very amusing, he thought.

He put his hand on her shoulder and kept it there.

"Well, I'm part of your job," he reminded her pleasantly, "and I'll expect a lot of attention. Altogether," he added, releasing her shoulder and walking toward the waiting bellboys, "it looks like a very large summer season. I'll be seein' you. Cocktails, at seven, in my suite. I'll be expecting you *alone!*"

CHAPTER V

Judith regarded Wallace's departing back with mixed emotions, a mingling of annoyance, anger, and a swift, rather cynical amusement, all touched with troubling uncertainty. But her further contemplation of the situation was interrupted by the appearance of an agitated girl whose trunk had not arrived and who simply couldn't find the head porter. Having disposed of her, and of a lonely and gangling youth who wondered timidly if Miss Gillmore would find someone to play tennis with him in the morning — "Perhaps you play," he added, eyeing her hopefully — Judith found that it was teatime and so left her desk for her immediate duties.

She found her "regulars" already at the end of the lounge by the great stone fireplace talking in apparent amity. She was able to remember that Mrs. Renwick took one lump and lemon, Mrs. Orson two lumps and cream, Mr. Smith nothing but straight tea medium strong. Other guests, drifting through the lounge, paused and came over for a cup, and Bill Martin appearing out of the blue greeted her casually.

"Tea?"

"Haven't time. Thanks just the same." But he lingered to speak to little Gertrude Miller, the convalescent youngster, and her mother, and before departing came over to the tea table again.

"Sure you won't have any?"

"Perfectly. I could go for a cookie though." He took one, bit into it reflectively. "I passed by a little while ago but you were so engrossed with the new arrival that you didn't see me."

"Which new arrival?"

"Lady, do not stall. The one and only Wallace," he answered.

Her problem returned to her with redoubled force and she looked up at Bill's engaging face hesitantly, wondering if it would be wise to ask his advice. But of course not. If she couldn't handle relatively minor things like this on her own she certainly wasn't fit for her job. Besides, Bill's attention was distracted by Betty, who came flying up to them, her blond curls in disorder and her youth and vitality almost overpowering.

"What, no tea! Hasn't she offered you any?" she demanded.

"Twice. I refused. I've got to get to my office. I have hours in" — he looked at his watch — "ten minutes."

"Then sit down and have your tea." Betty, catching him off guard, pushed him firmly into a big chair and sat down on the arm. "He likes his strong and straight," she informed Judith, "and I want mine weak with lemon. . . . Bill, I haven't seen you all day, you've neglected me shamefully," she accused him.

"My time is not my own, my little geranium," he said affectionately.

Judith gave them their tea. She felt shut out, alone. A little later, when most of the guests had gone, when Bill had gone off to his office with Betty clinging to his arm, she left the lounge to go to her room. But, on second thought, she knocked on the door of Mr. Corbin's office.

He was alone and welcomed her smiling. Judith went in and stood beside the desk.

"No, please don't get up," she said, "I won't take very much of your time. You'll think me rather foolish." She hesitated and flushed, looking, to his dismay and appreciation, even younger than Betty, "but I feel I must ask your advice about one thing and then I won't trouble you again."

"Fire away," he said cordially.

She told him of Wallace's invitation. "Not that it was an invitation really," she said ruefully; "it was more like a command performance. And honestly, Mr. Corbin, I don't know what to do. If I were here as a guest I could take it or leave it. But I'm not a guest." She paused, waiting, and he frowned a little and looked away.

"Bert Wallace," he said slowly, "is accustomed to having his own way. However, in this case your position is not quite that of just hotel hostess. You have known Wallace for a good many years. You are, in fact, old friends. When this comes up again — as it will of course innumerable times, and with innumerable guests — you will handle it in your own way. Tactfully, I am sure. There can always be some excuse. In this case frankly," he admitted, as if ashamed, "it's difficult for me to decide anything about Bert Wallace without prejudice, and I've been forced to overlook a good many things in his case. We — all of us who are concerned with the success of the hotel — are under the deepest obligation to his father . . . and Mr. Wallace, whom I count as a personal friend, is completely besotted about Bert. Bert is helpful to us too. He not only makes Rivermount his headquarters, but he brings people, either as his guests or on his recommendation. Nowadays," he added, "as you know as well as I, there is little food for scandal in an invitation to cocktails, even when the host is a young man and the guest a young woman. And in this case, as you are old friends —"

Judith went to her room, and ran the water for her bath. Dressing later, she contemplated herself in the mirror, the grave, oval face, the black eyes, the thick silken waves of red hair. She was on her own with a vengeance. Tacitly Mr. Corbin had given her leave to handle the importunities of any of his male guests as she pleased, so long as she was tactful about it . . . but Bert Wallace was apparently sacrosanct.

It wouldn't do to antagonize him at the outset, she thought unhappily. She believed she knew him well enough to know that such conduct on her part would make for a species of pleased persecution on his.

Well, she was free, white, and something over twenty-one. She would manage . . . him, herself, and her job.

She ran her reddest lipstick over her mouth, regarded her simple, excessively smart dinner frock with impersonal pleasure, and sat down to write to her mother. When she had finished, it was a little before seven.

Wallace's rooms were on the sixth, hers on the fifth. She walked up the flight of stairs, turned down a corridor and knocked. He opened the door, and stood there smiling at her, very correct and almost too good-looking in excellently tailored white flannels and a blue coat.

"Come in," he said heartily, "I've been waiting for you with the utmost impatience."

The Rivermount management had provided him with a pleasant apartment, a big living room, many windowed, filled with flowers and comfortably furnished. Off it, one assumed, a bedroom and bath. "Not a bad place," he told her carelessly. "Here, sit down."

Evidently he did not trust to the hotel's barkeeper, for the ingredients of a cocktail were on a small serving table with ice and a shaker. He mixed expertly, shook with abandon, poured her drink into a chilled glass, and passed her some tiny caviar sandwiches. Then he sat down beside her on the couch. "Well, here's mud in your eye," he said cheerfully, "and gold in your job. Like it?"

"It's very good," she said, tasting.

"Of course it is. But I meant the job, not the cocktail."

"I like it a lot," she told him, "so far."

Wallace finished his drink, set the glass down on the table, slid a careless arm along the back of the sofa.

"You're certainly going to enliven my summer," he told her. "I'll expect a lot of attention, Judy."

"You'll get all you're entitled to," she promised, smiling, "but by the looks of this weekend, your percentage won't be very large. Think how busy I'll be when the summer crowd starts coming!"

"I'm the summer crowd," he said complacently. "I'll be up every weekend more or less, and all of July and August. Here, let me fill your glass."

She shook her head.

"No, thanks. One's my limit."

"Come on, be a sport, celebrate our reunion."

She said amiably:

"If you don't mind, I'd rather not. I'm anxious to keep my job, Bert, and if I go reeling up to Mr. Corbin's table —"

"Nonsense, you're going to dine with me!"

She said quickly:

"Thanks, but I can't. Not tonight anyway. You see, Mr. Corbin has been kind enough to ask me to sit with him and Betty."

"Wants to take you out of circulation, does he?"

"Not at all. There'll often be lonely people who'll want me to —"

"How about me? I'm lonely," he said dramatically.

"You needn't be," she said, laughingly. "See here, Bert, don't you ever work?"

"Of course," he said, distracted, "like a slave. Oh, you mean the vacation." He laughed. "That's all set," he told her confidentially, refilling his glass, "and the office is delighted to get rid of me. I'm just a handsome figurehead as it is, as the old man's general manager is the big shot. I've a large room, all paneled, and a pretty secretary and I take customers out to lunch. That's my job. But during the summer there aren't so many to take out. So I expect to lure some of them up here for golf and a swim and good Scotch. That's my way of working and it's pretty damned effective, if I do say so."

"I've no doubt of it," agreed Judith without inflection.

Wallace looked up at her a little sharply, but her face was without expression.

She rose and smiled at him. "Thanks for the drink. I'll have to run along now, the Corbins are expecting me."

"What's your hurry?" He went with her to the door, slipped his arm about her. "How about a little kiss for old time's sake?" he inquired, holding her close.

Judith disengaged herself without much difficulty. Her heart was racing but her composure remained. She said, laughing:

"Honestly, Bert, is it my job that has altered you? We were never on kissing terms in the old days."

"We can remedy that," he said, "I didn't half appreciate you."

"My poverty," she said lightly, "invests me with a new glamour. That's it. I've become a glamour girl . . . on a salary."

"Don't put me off," he said, "you can't."

He was, she saw becoming interested and insistent. At first, perhaps, he'd been joking. Now he joked no longer. She thought swiftly and then said the first thing that occurred to her.

"Bert, hadn't you better be more cautious? After all, consider my position. I may be desperate. I may not like working really. Perhaps I've just taken this job in order to expedite my search for an eligible husband. You're the most eligible man here, you know."

She was unruffled, her eyes laughed at him. And young Mr. Wallace, who prided himself on being a confirmed bachelor, stepped back in very real alarm. He said uncertainly:

"Do you mean . . . ? Of course you don't! But . . ." He regarded her, puzzled, and she knew with amused certainty that from now on he would never be quite sure of her. "You're a cool one," he told her with unwilling admiration, "if that's really your game."

"Of course it is," she said, "it's every woman's, isn't it? Especially every poor woman's. You should thank me for the warning. 'Bye." She smiled again and was gone. He heard her walking down the corridor and he heard her laugh, very distinctly, as he closed the door.

Wallace returned to the cocktail shaker. He swore gently and ran a finger around the inside of his collar, which seemed a little too tight. What a girl! He was, he admitted to himself, a little afraid of her. But two could play at that game, and he wouldn't be the one to be hooked. He grinned at himself in a mirror over the serving table. Still, caution remained the byword.

He remembered Judy Gillmore when she had been of another world, his world. A pretty redheaded girl with plenty of spirit.

She had told him off properly that summer about Ruth — what was her name? — the silly little kid who'd visited her and fallen in love with him. Judy hadn't spared him and he hadn't liked it or her, very much. Nor had she held any special appeal for him once he'd granted her physical charm. Too frank, too outspoken, too — yes, he had to admit it, too damned well-bred. And she was still frank and outspoken, heaven knew, only now she was on her own.

She'd been a fool to tell him that, whether she meant it or not, he reflected, inclined to think that she *had* meant it. It might amuse him to warn other potential victims.

Judith, on her way to dinner, congratulated herself. She had, she thought, spiked young Mr. Wallace's guns rather neatly. It would have been no use to struggle, turn coy, plead her position, grow dramatic. He was of the type that thrived on struggles, pleas, drama. The girl of a couple of decades ago would have pointed out that he might be compromising her, cocktails for two in a hotel room, caviar and love-making. But to-day's daughter, Miss Gillmore, had but to point out that he might be compromising himself, and his ardor died as quickly as it had been born.

Corbin was alone at his table when she came in. He rose, and when she was seated and had given her order, regarded her with veiled anxiety.

"You . . . I mean . . . that is to say, you saw Bert Wallace?" he began.

"I had one drink," she said cheerfully. "I think when I left him he was pouring out his third. I stayed less than half an hour and everything was very amiable," she assured him. "Where's Betty?"

"She'll be along. She's always late. Went out after tea, somewhere. She misses her friends."

"They were nice kids," said Judith. "I was sorry to see them go. Here she comes now, with Bill Martin."

Betty was coming down the long arched room, her frail full skirts billowing about her slim waist, tugging along Bill Martin who hadn't, it was plain, dressed for dinner. She cried, when the table was reached:

"I persuaded Bill. It's so seldom he honors us. Judy, you look too divine." She sank into a chair and demanded a menu. "I'm starved," she said.

Bill grinned contritely at Corbin.

81

"I couldn't escape," he said. "This kid ought to be in Congress; she certainly knows how to sway an audience."

"You're always welcome," said Corbin cordially, "but as a rule you bolt your dinner and escape before we come in."

"Just a slave to humanity," murmured Bill. "After the tea which your child forced on me, and which never agrees with me, I had office hours. All of five patients from town. And then I was called upstairs to Mrs. Renwick."

"Anything serious?" asked Mr. Corbin anxiously.

"No," replied Bill, suppressing the desire to add *unfortunately*. "After which I returned to my office and immersed myself in a good book. Or perhaps I fell asleep. Anyway, my routine was thrown out of gear."

"I tried to get him to take me to the grill," said Betty.

"Can't afford it," Bill informed her calmly.

"Well, you can buy me a demitasse," she said, "and we'll dance."

"The exchequer," he agreed solemnly, "will just run to that."

Her father said gently, "You mustn't impose on Bill, Betty."

"It's not imposing. You know the gag about all work and no play. He'll be an old gentleman with a long gray beard if I don't work on him now and then. Besides, I'm dying to dance and Saks Lewis's orchestra is an inspiration."

"How about you?" Bill asked Judith. "Care to shake a hoof? I might run to three demitasses . . . and even a slice of pie."

Judith shook her head, smiling, for it was easy to read the anxious look which Betty shot at her: "Lay off," said the look very plainly, "and give me a break. After all, I saw him first!"

"I have some contract games to arrange," she said, "and then we're having movies tonight, you know."

One of the newly arrived guests, an old friend of the Corbins, came over to their table and sat down for a moment. After the introductions, he drew Corbin and Betty into conversation and Bill turned to Judith.

"You take your duties very seriously, don't you?" he murmured.

"Of course, why?" she demanded, astonished.

"Mrs. Renwick's room is on the sixth floor," he said ambiguously.

Judith flushed. He had seen her then, either going in or coming out of Wallace's room. She said hotly:

"I doubt if I owe you an explanation, but if you mean that Bert Wallace asked me up for a cocktail before dinner, what of it?"

"Oh, nothing," said Bill, shrugging, "more power to you. Only I warn you that is how our late lamented hostess lost her job, too many cocktails before dinner, too much favoritism and — taking too much for granted."

She said angrily:

"I've known you a couple of weeks —"

"You don't count knocking me over on a bicycle?" he interrupted sadly.

"I do not, and I've known Bert Wallace for years. And I'd be grateful if you'd —"

"Mind my own business? Well, that's a difficult thing to ask of anyone of my temperament and profession," he said. He looked across at Betty and smiled. "Well, youngster," he said good-naturedly, "let's get going if we're going to have that demitasse and a couple of dances . . . because I've a call to make at nine."

Corbin, his acquaintance departing at the same time, looked after Betty's straight back and smiled at Judith, not noting her preoccupation.

"I'm afraid," he said, "that my child's a little obvious. Poor Bill, he can't call his soul his own! She believes she's irrevocably in love with him and shouts it from the housetops. He's charming to her, treats her as if she were his younger sister and yet the position must be difficult for him. These modern youngsters —" he shook his head and laughed — "are perfectly shameless, they pursue openly. But Martin's a fine fellow. I don't suppose Betty's really serious about him; she'll fall in love a dozen times before she's twenty, yet if anything came of it I'd be extremely glad. I don't know anyone I'd like better in the family than Bill Martin. Don't be deceived by his casualness, Judy. He's a very clever and extremely ambitious young man."

She thought, And his ambition may include marrying the boss's daughter, not that Betty's father is really his boss, but —

Aloud she said, "They'd make a very attractive couple," and wondered wildly why she disliked the idea so much. Perhaps it was because Betty wasn't cut out to be a doctor's wife. Or was she? You couldn't tell about these crazy impulsive eighteen-year-olds. Very often they settled down in an early marriage and made competent and splendid wives.

Yet she still disliked the idea.

CHAPTER VI

The rest of the holiday weekend was so crowded that Judith had little time to speculate on Betty's pursuit of Bill Martin or on her own position in regard to Bert Wallace. She was busy, it seemed, every minute, arranging parties, card games, introductions, smoothing over annoyances, and meeting her first example of the hotel hostess's nightmare — the Problem Child. This first one was a tired young divorcée, up for the weekend and determined to make the most of it. Judith, not without malice, wished her on Bert Wallace, and he was at first nothing loath. At least there'd be no quarter given and taken, she decided, for Bert could look after himself and so could Mrs. Ellerton.

Mrs. Ellerton was a willowy blonde, slightly on the Garbo side, who, however, had no wish to be alone. She was still in love with her husband, she confided in Judith twenty minutes after their first meeting, but he had been reft from her by an unspeakable brunette. She named names with the utmost abandon. Not that he had married the wretch, she said hopefully, for it appeared that the unspeakable brunette wouldn't have him. He hadn't enough money now, what with the heavy but merited alimony. Mrs. Ellerton was of the practical opinion that one nail drives out another, so when she wasn't pursuing Judith to her very room, desirous of telling her her troubles — "You are so simpatico, as they say in Italy," she murmured — she was hounding Bert Wallace, on the golf links, at the stables, in the grillroom and the ballroom. And it amused him a little.

Judith found herself free to dance several times during the festivities. In fact, Bert, encountering her near the ballroom, dragged her there with a firm hand. "It's a hostess's duty," he said, "to find partners for the wallflowers."

"Since when have you come under that category?"

"Just this minute. What was the idea of sicking the Ellerton onto me, you little fiend?"

"Don't you like her?"

"Oh, immensely, but she cloys. I've promised to drive her to Lover's Leap tonight when the moon is full. For a half a dollar I'd push her over." He tightened his arm about Judith. "Aren't you a little alarmed?" he inquired. "The hotel will be overrun with Ellertons during the season, you'll have lots of competition!"

"I love competition," she said gaily.

The ballroom, an immense affair, was by no means crowded. The night was unusually warm for that time of year in the mountains and couples kept drifting to the big verandas. Firmly Judith resisted any attempt on Wallace's part to follow them. "You asked me to dance," she said, "and dance I will." When the music stopped they were standing near the orchestra platform and Betty was there too, talking to the young leader. Bill Martin was, of course, nowhere to be seen and Betty, far from forlorn as she had plenty of partners, was amusing herself making big eyes at "Sax" and asking him clearly, "Don't you ever get a chance to dance too?"

"That kid," mused Wallace aloud, "has possibilities."

Judith felt a tiny clutch of alarm about her heart. Worse medicine for a rattle-brained but essentially sweet eighteen-year-old than Bert Wallace could not possibly be imagined. Still, so far as anyone could see, Betty had no eyes for anyone but Bill Martin . . . except the pair she was now using on Saks Lewis, with decided effect.

The music began a number for which Betty had asked. She whirled back to her partner, a boy not much older than herself, and Judith drifted into Wallace's arms again. "Just this one," she told him. "I have to keep a date with one of my old ladies and meantime Mrs. Ellerton is looking for you, there in the archway. The moon must be rising," she added a trifle maliciously.

"Come with us," he begged. "For the first time in my life I crave a chaperon!"

But she declined, laughing, and a little later was walking across the veranda to the cardroom, where she had promised to meet Mrs. Orson for a game of Russian bank, when she saw Bill Martin, standing outside the windows, smoking and looking in. The chatter, the laughter and music came clearly to them out there, the bright dresses of the women were very charming, and the soft warm air relaxing.

"Peri at the gates of Paradise?" she inquired, pausing. "Why don't you go in and dance?"

He threw away his cigarette.

"You're far too educated for me," he said, grinning. "No, thanks, not even with you. And have you forgotten me?"

"I didn't mean me," she said indignantly. "Betty's there — and our weekend beauty,

Mrs. Ellerton. And there's nothing to forgive."

"Thanks, I've met the lady. She had a headache last evening," he reported without enthusiasm. "No, ma'am, I'm going to bed. I went out on a case just before dinner, in the village. And I'm dog-tired."

She said, "You haven't had anything to eat, have you?"

"A cup of coffee in the farmhouse kitchen . . . I just got back. But I left a ten-pound boy behind me at the Ralstons', so I've something to show for my dinnerless state."

"The grill's open," she suggested.

"But the main dining room's closed," he told her. "Lady, I have no money to squander on chicken sandwiches at nine p.m. . . . Why aren't you dancing?"

"I'm off to play Russian bank," she said. "Good night, Bill."

But in the cardroom she stopped to telephone to the grill and order sandwiches and coffee sent to Dr. Martin's room, the check to be charged to her. After all, she reflected, shuffling the cards, her expenses were very light and she could afford to be a girl scout once in a blue moon.

When she reached her room shortly before eleven, having escorted Mrs. Orson to hers and seen that the hot-water bottles, without which in the night Mrs. Orson froze, were at the right temperature, she found a note stuck under her door. The writing was completely unfamiliar and even her name was hard to read. Standing there beside the desk at the window, a single lamp throwing its circle of yellow light, she read:

"Thanks for the charity, lady. I'll get even. How about lunch Tuesday — isn't that your day off?"

She went to bed smiling a little, wondering how he knew.

That was Sunday. Monday the exodus began. By Tuesday morning the hotel would be empty again, but on Thursday two conventions were coming in. Usually from Monday midmorning until after dinner Judith was free. She had not been taking her time off regularly, merely an hour or so on her free days, in her own room writing or reading or else walking to the village for magazines or to stop and see her friends. This week she had changed to Tuesday; she would relax, she'd have tea with Mr. Alcot, she might even take the Valleytown bus, dine in lonely state and see a movie.

Bill called her before breakfast.

"Sorry to get you up," he said. "I didn't have a glimpse of you yesterday, I was at the hospital most of the day. Look, what are your plans for today?"

She told him.

"Good. I'll pick you up at Hank's around twelve and we'll have some lunch. Then I'll take you with me on my calls. I've got to be back here for office hours, but I'm going over to the hospital early in the evening, and if you'd overlook my reckless driving . . ."

"Don't be silly," she said, "I think I can hold you down."

At noon she was gossiping comfortably with Prudence in the Parsons' kitchen when Bill clattered in without ceremony. "Come and git it," he announced, hugging Prudence and clucking foolishly at the cat which seemed to know him, "we're going on a picnic."

"Picnic?"

"No spikka da English? I stopped at the Daisy Diner, and got us some sandwiches and a thermos of coffee. I told you I'd get even."

"You'll die," said Prudence severely, seized a newly frosted cake, cut it in half, took waxed paper from a drawer and made a neat parcel. "Here, you two loons," she said affectionately.

They drove out to Hillhigh Falls. It had been a long time since Judith had been there, to sit on a flat rock warm with the sun and watch the narrow white ribbon of the falls unwinding itself over the rocks. Pines and spruce, hemlock and cedar were thick and green about her, the little river chattered noisily below, the deciduous trees were in delicate leaf, there were patches of violets at her feet and over her head the cloudless blue sky.

She sat down and put her hands among the brown fallen needles, aromatic and slippery. She sighed, tossed her hat aside and folded her hands in her lap. "This is very nearly heaven!"

"I know. I don't have much chance to come here now," Bill said, pouring the coffee and unpacking the sandwiches. "Golly, these are thick, think you can open your mouth wide enough, Judy? . . . But when I was a kid the Home used to bring us here now and again."

"Don't talk," she said suddenly, biting into a sandwich. "I mean, we hear so much talking, don't we, both of us?"

He gave her a surprised, appreciative look and said rather thickly, "Bad manners anyway. Got enough mustard?"

Judith nodded, and they ate and drank in a companionable silence. Later, when the crumbs had been cleared away and the papers disposed of, he said, lying full length on his stomach:

"I'd forgotten how lovely it was here until yesterday."

"I thought you were at the hospital yesterday."

"I was. But in the afternoon I came back to the office. My one patient broke the Monday appointment. So Betty persuaded me to ride with her. I haven't ridden in years . . . not since I worked for old man Kinton one summer and rode his horses bareback all over the fields. I wasn't any too good but at least I stayed put, and I'm sore as the devil today," he admitted, laughing.

"Betty's a sweet kid," said Judith slowly.

"Yes, isn't she?" He was perfectly casual. "Sometimes I'd like to put her across my knee and spank her, but she's all right. Alex has done a good job . . . and it must have been difficult. She's going back to school this week to graduate."

"Yes, I know."

He wasn't in love with the child, he couldn't speak so casually if he were. But now he was saying, "I'll miss her, she's fun to have around." Then he looked at his watch, whistled, jumped to his feet.

"Come on," he said, "let's get going, we've work to do."

They made his rounds and he later dropped her at Mr. Alcot's where she had tea in the garden and sat with the gentle old man until dusk, feeling refreshed and re-created by her day, away from people who buzzed and clamored, away from the pressure, the sense of hurry, the anxiety lest something go wrong. The long golden shadows crept closer, these early June days were brimmed with a lavish beauty. And then, just before dark, Bill's horn honked imperiously and she went out to meet him.

They drove toward Valleytown, the busy little manufacturing center, and had dinner at a farmhouse which served marvelous meals, just on the town's outskirts. After that, replete, they went on to the hospital and Judith waited while Bill went in. He was gone for almost an hour and was apologetic when he came out.

"Gee, I'm sorry," he said, "but —"

"I've been asleep," she confessed, "and you needn't apologize."

He said contritely:

"But I do. I thought we'd take in a movie — there's a good one in town — but I called the hotel just now and there was a message for me. Betty's hurt her ankle, I've got to get back."

"Oh, poor kid," said Judith, sitting up, "she may not be able to go back to school."

"It may be just a sprain. If it's a break . . . Well, there isn't a portable X-ray anywhere in these parts. I wish I could afford my own," he said irritably. "I'll have to bring her back to the hospital. Hold your hat, we're on our way."

His anxiety was, she assured herself, merely that of the friend as well as physician. Or was it? She was quiet most of the way home and when he had parked the car and jumped out, she asked, "Can't I help?"

"No, I'll go see her now. You deserve your day off." He looked at her and smiled. "It was a swell day," he told her and was up the steps and into the house ahead of her, hurrying toward his patient.

She followed him slowly. She told herself in a fury of rebellion, I can't fall in love with him. Where would it get us, even if he were in love with me too? I haven't a cent. Young penniless doctors can't afford penniless wives. If he has any sense he'll fall in love with Betty if he isn't already. Alex Corbin has enough to help them. They could live at the hotel. Oh, why *am* I such a fool? I've been here only three weeks and I've fallen in love with one of the most exasperating men I've ever known and certainly, she added, thinking of what she had told Bert Wallace, certainly the most ineligible!

She did not feel any of the flutters and fancies and dawning glows of fiction. Having admitted that she was in love, she felt angry with herself and extraordinarily tired. It's just the silly season, she assured herself fiercely. In another couple of weeks this place will be full to the doors and I'll forget all about it. I'm lonely, that's all.

But she had a vision of Bill bending over Betty, touching her ankle with careful, competent, tender fingers, and her eyes filled with foolish tears and she fumbled putting her key in its lock. If Bert Wallace hadn't gone back to town, she told herself furiously, she'd call his room and ask him to take her out some place, where they could dance and laugh and fence with each other. She knew where she stood with Bert. As for Bill Martin, she loved him, and she wished that she had never seen him, that she had not come to Rivermount.

Of course, she thought, lying listlessly across her bed, I can give up the job.

CHAPTER VII

When on Wednesday morning Judith woke after a brief, deep sleep, the back of her neck felt poker-stiff with tension and her eyes were heavy. But the sun shone, birds sang like mad from the tall trees, and beyond her window she could see the superb calm of the mountains and the silver winding of the river. Morning brings light in more than the ordinary sense. Hurrying to get ready for breakfast she thought scornfully, How could I be such an idiot? I wouldn't give up my job for any man on earth. I've got it, I'll hang on to it.

She turned embarrassed mental eyes from the spectacle of herself last night. Loneliness, that was all; propinquity. A hundred and one trivial things merging to appear as an alarming whole. If she didn't succeed in arguing herself out of having fallen in love with young Dr. Martin, she could at least try to believe that it wasn't serious, that it would pass. And if this be love, this memory of torment, this self-scorn and — yes — irritation at herself, she wanted none of it!

Judith had never before been in love. She had liked one or two men very much indeed, and during her first uprooted months in Chicago she had felt a strong pull of attraction toward one of the cheerful penniless young men she had met at Aunt Emily's — Jack Thomson, a nice boy, with more looks than brains, a great fund of gaiety and good humor. He had been, by his own admission, crazy about her. She had gone out with him a few times, dining at a cheap table-d'hôte place and going to a movie afterward. But she hadn't for a moment entertained the idea of marrying him — any more than he had dreamed of marrying her. He was set to marry the boss's daughter, he informed her gaily at the outset of their acquaintance, but unfortunately he changed bosses often and most of them didn't have daughters . . . unmarried ones anyway.

Judith had never deluded herself that the interest she'd felt in Jack was serious. Perhaps she could talk herself out of this one too as time went on . . . time, they say, cures everything. But she wasn't certain. How do you know the real thing, she inquired, looking at herself in the mirror, how does anyone know? Certainly she hadn't experienced any of the fictional requirements. Her knees hadn't turned to water, her hands hadn't grown cold and her cheeks hot when Bill walked by or stopped to speak to her. She had felt, well, merely stimulated, keyed up — and in a strange way, familiar with her own emotions, as if she had experienced all this before or had been expecting it. Yesterday at the Falls she had merely felt content, with a deep happiness to which she couldn't give a name, as if it were right that they should be together, not talking much, just close and quiet and content.

And then, she thought ashamed, all this soul searching. All this *if* business. If he loved me, if we were married! How literally absurd. He hadn't a thought for her. If he thought about anyone it was probably Betty Corbin, and Judith wasn't sure even of that. It was a good thing he couldn't read minds as well as he — probably — took pulses. How horrified and embarrassed he would have been!

Well, it would pass. Other women had fallen in love and recovered, not once, but several times. Meantime it was June, she had a job, conventions were coming in . . . and she must hurry to breakfast, find out how Betty was and if she could do anything, and then get to work.

She had not slept much, except toward morning, and her eyes were startlingly shadowed against her pallor. She touched her cheekbones lightly with rouge, used her lipstick to advantage, selected one of her simple, beautifully cut cotton frocks and went to breakfast. Mr. Corbin had breakfasted and gone and the pleasant waitress told her that she understood poor Betty had broken her ankle and was in the hospital.

After coffee, orange juice and dry toast — which was all she could manage, although the waitress asked, "You aren't dieting, Miss Gillmore, are you . . . not with your figure?" — Judith made her way to Corbin's office, halted briefly en route by a girl who wanted to play tennis — and with whom she promised to play at eleven, and finally reached his door.

"How's Betty?" she wanted to know, coming in.

He told her that he and Bill had taken her right over to the hospital last night for an X-ray and then the fracture had been reduced. The foot was in a cast and she must remain in the hospital for a little while. It wasn't a bad break at all; in fact, Bill had told her that she would probably have less trouble with it eventually than if she had torn the ligaments. She would be home in a few days but she wouldn't be able to return to school for graduation. He had just had the headmistress on the telephone and she had assured him that Betty's work warranted that she be given a diploma *in absentia.* So that was that. He was sorry, he said ruefully; it meant she wouldn't be able to play tennis or golf, ride or swim for a while. But they'd try to make it up to her.

"She'll be lonely," said Judith, "perhaps I can sneak off and go see her sometime today."

Corbin was going right after lunch, he said, and if Judith was free he'd be glad to take her.

From then on Judith's time was very full. The conventions came and went and the summer guests arrived bag and baggage, young and old, male and female, thin and fat, pleasant and unpleasant. Judith was more than busy. For the week that Betty remained in the hospital she managed to run over every day either with the girl's father or with Bill Martin. Then Betty came home, still in the cast. But her good little bones knitted rapidly and, while for some time she was barred from active sports, she was soon very much herself again.

Bert Wallace arrived, on the dot, in his plane, for long weekends. On the first weekend following their brief encounter in his rooms his behavior toward Judith was practically exemplary. She arranged a picnic for him, and a motorboat excursion. He was suitably grateful but regarded her, she thought with a flicker of inner amusement, with suspicion. But after that weekend his vigilance relaxed.

Hers was heightened. The summer visitors brought their problems. There were the usual parties of women and children, young, half-grown or grown, who milled about aimlessly seeking amusement during the week and then straightened up and were gay and dashing when Fridays came and the husbands arrived. There were visiting young men from Friday to Sunday and the girls bloomed like flowers. Nothing is more manless than a summer resort from Monday to Friday. There were sudden friendships, more sudden enmities, and an entirely different atmosphere during the major part of the week. Then there were married couples who came for the season or for vacations. Judith soon learned to distinguish the weekend or all-summer male who was very pleasant to her when his wife wasn't around, and not so pleasant when she was, from the reckless gentleman who had an eye for a pretty girl at any time of day, wife notwithstanding. These were the cases that called for tact and plenty of it.

"How about sneaking off and having a little drink with me?" was one approach, the gentleman in question usually very gay in sport togs, his hair thinning and his waistline thickening. He didn't have to add that his wife was playing golf or bridge.

Judith found that she could always offer an excuse and one that was legitimate: she had to work; she had to chaperon a picnic; she had to go into the village for old Mrs. So-and-so. And she usually ended by smiling cordially and confessing that she didn't drink during the day — "It makes me sleepy" — but that some evening perhaps before dinner she would be glad to join him and Mrs. This-or-that in a cocktail. There was nothing at which the importunate gentleman could take offense but he was put, very nicely, in his place. Bill, stopping at her desk just after one such encounter, congratulated her. "You are," he said, grinning, "marvelous. Why don't you write a book, a sort of hotel hostess Emily Post?"

"You get going," she retorted. "I haven't

time for idle flattery."

They were very good friends, she had that much to comfort her. He had never mentioned Bert Wallace . . . not since he had asked her if she had forgiven him, and she knew it was because of his comment concerning that too hospitable young man. Bill's attitude toward her was one of amused, admiring friendliness. Half a loaf was better than no bread. If she didn't see him too much, if she kept busy and occupied, loving him couldn't hurt her. Well, even if it hurt her it wouldn't hurt anyone else.

Toward the end of June Corbin called her into his office and she went with some trepidation. Wherein had she failed, now that the real test had come and that she was asked to manage and handle so many people? And over the Fourth of July there would be crowds.

"I'm worried about Betty," he said abruptly.

"But her ankle's fine."

"I don't mean that. She's all right physically. But that orchestra leader . . ."

"Oh, Saks!" Judith laughed. "He's an awfully nice boy," she said, and didn't stop to remember that he was, if anything, older than herself.

"No doubt. But she's getting herself talked about. I didn't think anything of it, when she couldn't dance, and used to sit up there on the platform and amuse herself, but —"

"Oh," said Judith, "you know the rocking-chair brigade! They'll talk about anyone and anything. I wouldn't worry if I were you. Saks is all right if a little on the temperamental side. And Betty's just young. I'll keep an eye on her if I can do it without her knowing." She drew a deep breath. "I was terrified when I knocked," she admitted. "I thought perhaps you weren't satisfied with the way I was working out."

"Nonsense, you're doing a great job. And perhaps I'm over-anxious about the child. But she doesn't confide in me — I don't suppose I have any reason to expect her to — and I thought she might have talked to you."

Judith was thoughtful. Betty's youthful exuberance and confidences no longer existed so far as Judith was concerned. She hadn't realized it until now, it had been unimportant, and there was so much else to concern her. But, thinking back, she remembered that while the youngster remained perfectly friendly toward her she had changed since shortly after her return

106

from the hospital. Why? Had she, then, something to conceal?

There was no one whom she could discuss it with except Bill, and Bill was the last person.

On the weekend before July Fourth, Bert Wallace arrived for his long vacation. He brought three men with him in the plane and two more came by train to join his party over the holiday. "God's gift to women," said Bill Martin to Judith as they stood together on the lookout over the water and watched Bert and his guests disporting themselves, for the swimming season was in full swing. "He's gladdened the heart of a dozen pretty girls, not to mention the married women, by bringing his entourage along."

"You don't like him much, do you?" asked Judith.

"I've no special reason to," said Bill shortly, "but I'm under heavy obligation to his father. Golly, who's that!" he demanded, staring.

A rather tall, elegantly slim brunette was walking down the steps leading to the bathhouses and piers. She wore a brief suit and her skin was the golden brown of perfectly done pancakes. She wore a scarlet silk handkerchief far back on black curls and tied under her chin. She waved at Judith and smiled, and even at that distance Bill could see that her eyes were enormous, her mouth very red and her teeth very good.

"Ain't dat sumpin'?" he murmured. "I hope she gets some minor ailment very soon."

"New arrival," explained Judith, suppressing a desire to smack him. "Her name is Miss Candace Howland. She's registered from Washington, D.C. She has a suite on the fourth floor, and is to be here until after Labor Day."

"Alone?"

"Well, she came alone," said Judith, laughing, "but the indications are that she'll have plenty of companionship."

She couldn't quite place Miss Howland herself. Looks, supreme; clothes, judging from the traveling suit of dark silk and the little hat, all right. One couldn't judge from sun suits. Manner, perfect, almost too perfect. Inflection, well-bred, almost too well-bred. Jewels, so far not many, but those Judith had seen were impeccable, a good small string of pearls and a fine cat's-eye ring. Age, anything from twenty-five to thirty-two. Skin, marvelous. She had brought a personal maid, a Pekinese dog and plenty of luggage. Judith, apprised in advance of her arrival, had sent the usual flowers and note to her suite and Miss Howland had stopped at her desk to thank her. She thought, she said, smiling, that she was going to like Rivermount very much. A friend had told her about it.

"I've got to get back to the hotel," Judith now said reluctantly. "I've promised to chaperon a party of teenagers on a picnic."

"Think I'll go down and take a look at the swimmers," said Bill carelessly. "I haven't anything to do for all of fifteen minutes."

"She should be a knockout in a bathing suit," said Judith coldly.

He grinned and said, "Jealous little thing, aren't you? Don't forget we have a date for Monday," and was off, running down the steps.

On her way to the hotel Judith passed an old-fashioned pergola overgrown with vines, from which Betty Corbin's voice reached her quite clearly.

"Of course I like you," she was saying, with a hint of exasperation, "but —"

"It's Martin," said her companion, and Judith recognized Saks Lewis's voice. "You make an idiot of yourself over him. Everyone knows that. And everyone knows that

Judith Gillmore —"

Judith, scarlet to her small ears, fled. Her heart thumped in her breast. Everyone knew *what?* That Judith Gillmore was making a fool of herself over him too?

She was at her desk talking to the housekeeper when Betty came into the lounge, flipped a hand at her and would have passed her had Judith not called her. She came rather reluctantly, and Mrs. Jarvis went on with her duties.

"Look," said Judith coaxingly, "won't you come on the picnic today? It's going to be fun, several carloads. We're going to the Falls," she added with some reluctance. It hurt her to plan for parties at the Falls. "And I'm rounding up everyone who's young and lively."

"I'll go," said Betty, "if Saks can come too. He can bring his accordion and we'll all sing. I'm bored stiff with the crowd around here, but Saks is pretty exciting."

"There's no reason why he shouldn't come," said Judith evenly, "there'll be other boys along. What about the band?"

"Most of 'em went into Valleytown this morning," said Betty, "they all get fed up hanging round waiting to play. I can't blame them, this is the dullest summer I ever spent," she added petulantly.

"It's hardly begun," Judith reminded her.

"Well, it can't be over too soon for me," said Betty, looking down at the older girl.

Judith said gently:

"I like Saks a lot, he's all right. But your father is a little bothered about him, Betty, and you —"

"I wish Dad would mind his own business," said Betty furiously, "and you too, Judy. I'm not a child. I'm eighteen" — She drew herself to her full height of five foot two — "and I can manage my own affairs, thank you, and I should think you'd have enough of your own to worry about without barging in on mine."

Her voice broke and she was very close to tears. She turned and ran off, almost colliding with Bert Wallace.

"Well, what's wrong with the infant?" he demanded, smiling.

"Nothing," said Judith shortly. "I thought you were in swimming."

"I was, but I came out, some few minutes ago. Have an important phone call to make. Judy, when are you going to let me take you up for a hop?"

"Oh, I don't know," she said, "sometime when I'm not busy."

"You're always busy, aren't you?" he

said, staring down at her. His eyes were the lightest blue she had ever seen. "But you have days off — Mondays, aren't they? How about spending next Monday with me? We'll drive out somewhere, have some lunch. Go up for a hop in the afternoon and find something really amusing to do in the evening."

She had pledged herself to Bill for Monday. She had spent part of every Monday with him since that first time. But now, remembering Saks Lewis's careless words, she said, "All right, Bert, but how about making it a party? I mean . . ."

"We'll see about that," he said. "By the way, that's a very good-looking gal who just made her appearance on the dock. Scarlet bathing suit. Five-alarm fire, that's what she is. Old Mrs. Dillon presented me; it seems they came up on the train together. I've asked her to come up for cocktails tonight . . . along with half a dozen others. You too, of course. Sevenish."

He disappeared in the direction of the elevator and Judith stared after him. Why had she committed herself to going out with him on Monday? But she knew why. Still, she wished she hadn't. But perhaps by Monday, she reflected hopefully, he would have changed his plans

CHAPTER VIII

On Monday morning she stopped in at Bill's office. Its equipment was secondhand, but adequate, and when she walked in Bill was barking at someone over the telephone. "Well, see that it's done," he was shouting. "When I leave an order I mean it to be carried out."

He hung up and glared at her.

"The stupidity of people!" he announced. "I could fry 'em in oil. That poor kid! All because an ignorant mother —" He broke off, ran his hand through his dark hair and grinned at her. "Sorry," he said contritely. "Look here. Judith, I may be late for our lunch date."

She said calmly, "That's what I came about. I'm sorry, Bill. I forgot that I'd promised Bert Wallace —"

"Okay by me," he said, before she had finished. "Far be it from me to stand in your way. The season's short and you've got to work fast."

She said furiously, "I don't know what you're talking about!"

"If you don't you're a lot dumber than I

think you are. Lunch at the Daisy Diner or sandwiches for two along some country road and waiting in the old bus while I make my calls must have palled on you long ago. Wallace has a fast car and a fat purse." He rose and slammed his roll-top desk shut. "No hard feelings," he said, not looking at her. "Any time you haven't anything better to do just call on me."

He picked up his bag, brushed past her and out the door, leaving her standing there between anger and astonishment. But after a moment laughter filled her eyes and her heart warmed. He must care for her, he couldn't possibly behave like that if he didn't. Her eyes fell on the desk again and on the picture of Betty standing on top of it, a framed snapshot with "All my love, Betty" scrawled across it.

Judith shrugged her slender shoulders and moved toward the door. Half a minute ago she had been inclined to run after him, to cry, "Bill, don't be silly, I didn't mean it. I don't want to go out with Bert Wallace, I'll tell him that I can't."

But now she compressed her lips and went slowly from the office, shutting the door behind her. If that was what he thought of her . . .

Bert had not asked anyone else. He was

waiting for her and his low-slung car was as polished as a jewel. Candace Howland, walking down the steps, smiled at them, "Have a nice time, you two," she said cordially. And as the car drove away Judith looked at Wallace.

"You might have asked her," she said.

"I may mix my drinks. But never my dates," he said firmly. "She and I are going fishing tomorrow. I've hired a boat for the season."

"You're a fast worker," said Judith, laughing, and leaned back, luxuriating in her freedom from the hotel, in the soft rush of air, in the glorious July sunlight and in a moment almost forgetting her companion.

Passing Miss Hetty Martin's house, they were halted by a shout. The old woman was leaning over the fence. "Hey, you," she called without ceremony.

"Stop, do," said Judith, amazed, and the car slid to a stop with a great screeching of brakes.

Miss Hetty came to the point without ceremony. "He's tall," she said, pointing to Bert, "and my cat's up the elm, drat her. I hauled out the ladder but I got dizzy."

Wallace raised his eyebrows but Judith was climbing out of the car. "Come on,

Bert," she called, "remember — one good deed a day."

"Will I be rewarded?" he inquired, following her.

"It ain't worth a cent more than a dime," said Miss Hetty, who had very sharp ears, "and you don't look as if you *needed* a dime, young man!"

Judith laughed at Wallace's confusion. He muttered something, and with Judith followed Miss Hetty's short quick steps to the tree against which the ladder leaned crazily. Above the top step, stretched along a branch, a mammoth tortoise-shell cat regarded the proceedings with indifference.

Wallace, resigned, took off his coat and climbed the ladder. Judith held it, looking up. The sunlight, scattered in green and gold through the leaves, fell upon her hair. And the old woman, standing by, her hands folded under her apron asked abruptly:

"Ain't I seen you before?"

"Of course, Miss Hetty," Judith answered. "I'm Judith Gillmore. I used to come here, summers. And one day your cat — it wasn't this one, was it? — got into trouble with a stray dog and —"

"I thought so," said Miss Hetty with satisfaction, "I knew it. Only person who ever

116

bothered to raise a hand. No, it ain't this cat, that one was his father, peskiest fighter I ever owned, and I've owned seventeen, all told. I've seen you, going by with — with —"

"With your nephew," supplied Judith, calmly watching Bert's efforts to coax the cat within reach.

"No nephew of mine," denied the old woman sharply; "takes after his mother, all her blood, rattle-brained . . ."

"Look out," cried Judith, "you'll never get him that way!"

"I can't reach her," shouted Bert, exasperated. "And I can't get out on that limb. Too far from the ladder."

"Then come down," ordered Judith, ignoring Miss Hetty's clamor, "and I'll go up."

He came gladly, but ordering that she do no such thing. "Want to break your neck?" he asked.

"I won't," she told him, "and you can't get anywhere with a cat by shouting at it." She turned to Miss Hetty, who looked more like a witch than ever, her face like a brown crabapple and her hair in wild disorder, "Have you any sardines?" she inquired.

"What would I be doing with them?" demanded Miss Hetty crossly. "Think I'm made of money?" Then she relented. "I've got an old fish head," she admitted. "Saved it for the cat."

Bert made a face and Judith shuddered but stood her ground. "Then let me have it," she said firmly.

Miss Hetty darted around to her back door and Bert, leaning against the tree said, "You mean to tell me you're going to climb up there?"

"With a fish head," said Judith firmly. "And without shouting. No self-respecting cat would come with someone bellowing 'Here, kitty' in a basso profundo in its ear!"

Miss Hetty returned. She had the fish head on a cracked china plate and, despite its pungent aroma, Judith seized it. "Mind you hold the ladder," she warned.

Bert, reluctant and disapproving, held it, while Judith climbed to the top, steady in her low and rubber-heeled oxfords. She spoke softly and enticingly to the animal, which eyed her with interest, its whiskers quivering slightly as the fish head began to make its presence known.

Still talking, Judith retreated slowly down the ladder. Before she had reached the third step pussy was on the first and so, majestically stalking her and the fish head, reached the ground in safety.

Judith presented the cat with the reward and scratched its head. Then she smiled at Miss Hetty. "May I wash my hands in your kitchen?" she asked.

The kitchen, unlike Miss Hetty herself, was spotlessly clean. The table was covered with a red-checked cloth. There was a potted geranium on the window sill. Copper, brass and aluminum were scoured. The sink was shining.

Judith washed the remains of the fish head from her fingers and dried her hands on a paper towel. Miss Hetty watched her. She said grudgingly, "You're a nice girl. Like cats, do you?"

"I love 'em," said Judith sincerely.

"Working up at the hotel now, ain't you?" pursued Miss Hetty.

Miss Hetty, it appeared, was not above making inquiries. "I am, and I like it very much," Judith said.

"Who's he?" inquired Miss Hetty with a jerk of her head in the general direction of her front yard.

"Oh," said Judith, "you know Bert Wallace, Miss Hetty, you've seen him most of his life, he grew up around here, summers."

"Oh, him! Nasty thieving boy he was," remarked Miss Hetty, "and probably no better since he grew up. Thought you were keeping company with — with Bill Martin."

Judith flushed.

"Young doctors just starting out can't afford to keep company," she said gaily.

"Why not?" demanded Miss Hetty sharply. "You ain't the kind of a girl who's afraid of hard work no matter how much you had once, are you? No, I thought not. Boy's a bigger fool than I took him for. Don't say you saw me or that I spoke about him," she ordered, as Judith went toward the door, "wouldn't have him think I'm interested. I ain't. Stop by again whenever you've a mind to. I bake on Saturdays. Like gingerbread cookies?"

Judith nodded and to her amazement found one in her hand, the big soft kind. She bit into it, exclaimed and smiled at the odd little woman. "It's marvelous," she said.

"They're good," admitted Miss Hetty. She walked through the yard with Judith, looked with disapproval at Bert leaning against the picket fence, and said, "Much obliged about the cat."

"It was nothing," Judith assured her and went out to the car. Bert followed, grumbling.

120

"Of all the nonsensical —"

"She hasn't anything to care for except the cat," said Judith, "I'm glad we happened by."

"Who in the world is she?"

"Surely you remember her, Bert? Miss Hetty Martin. She used to keep the sweet shop."

"Good Lord, I should say I do. We raided her once, a bunch of us kids. My father paid up afterward, very liberally, but she never forgave us. Say, isn't she some relation to our hotel doctor?"

"His aunt. But she won't admit it," said Judith.

"She's crazy as a coot," declared Bert, "and he ought to have her committed."

"She's not in the least crazy," said Judith, "and Bill wouldn't be such a fool as to try."

"You and he are pretty good friends, aren't you?"

"Of course."

"Why of course?" asked Bert negligently, heading the car away from Hillhigh. "Surely you're not considering him as one of your — eligible men?"

"I refuse to answer," said Judith lightly, "on the grounds that it might incriminate and degrade me."

"Know all the answers, don't you?" inquired Bert. "Yes, I'm beginning to think that you do."

"Oh, stop talking," said Judith, "and let me enjoy the drive. Where are we going, by the way?"

"To Little Lake. They built an inn there last year . . . remember? Oh, I forgot you wouldn't know about it. Nice little place, fair food . . ."

Little Lake was high in the mountains, round as a dollar, blue as the sky, fringed with tall pines. The inn was small, comfortable and not very crowded that day. They lunched on the screened porch looking out on the water. The food was simple and good and Judith shook her head when Bert suggested a drink.

"Not in the middle of the day," she began mechanically, and then laughed.

"I think that's funny," he admitted, "but why should you?"

"It's just because I've had to repeat it so often," she told him, "and if you're going to take me up in your plane you'd better confine yourself to one snifter, my good man."

"Okay darling," he said carelessly, "just as you say. Like flying, ever been up?"

"I love it. Yes, I've been up lots . . . but

not recently." Her face was clouded. "I flew to the coast once," she said; "Father was fit to be tied. But I was always crazy about it."

"Like to learn? I'll teach you."

She shook her head.

"No, thanks," she said, "a crack-up wouldn't help me with my job any. I'm content to let the other fellow do the flying."

"You take no risks with me, my girl," he said complacently, and then leaning a little closer, "That is to say, not in a plane."

His boast was not idle. He was an excellent pilot, sure, steady and controlled. They drove back to the hotel field and his ship was tuned up and waiting for him. He looked her over himself before they took off.

It was a luxurious cabin plane, four-passenger. Judith leaned back in the comfortable chair and watched the world unroll below her. Lakes like drops of water, rivers like trickles, and as they climbed the earth became a checkerboard and the mountains molehills. If you could only get out of yourself, she thought, in your daily life and see yourself amid your little world from such a perspective, an airplane view . . .

She was sorry when Bert brought them down to earth again. But he assured her it was time; their dinner date was some thirty miles away . . . and if she wanted to dress . . .

She did, she told him, much as she hated the flight to end. But he promised her "There will be others. All you want. You're a perfect passenger, you know . . . no giggles or panics or worries or questions."

Back at the hotel she went to her room, indulged in a long and luxurious bath and put on one of her prettiest frocks, the starched white cotton lace. With it she wore her great-grandmother's necklace of carved rosy coral and the coral button earrings. When she was ready she swept herself a curtsy in the long mirror. "You look, if I may say it, very attractive, Miss Gillmore," she murmured.

If only it weren't Bert —

She caught up a little taffeta cape and her evening bag and went out into the corridor. She was to meet Bert in the lounge. On her way there she encountered Bill, looking unshaven and a little haggard. He carried the inevitable bag and walked slowly as if he were dead tired.

"Dressed to kill," he commented, stopping.

"What an expression!"

"I meant it. Diana, before the hunt." He laughed shortly. "Had a nice day as far as you've gone?"

"Perfect." She was angry and he mustn't know it. "We spent the first part of it rescuing your aunt's cat from an elm."

"My aunt's!"

"In person. And then we had lunch at Little Lake. Then we went for an airplane ride."

"Lay off that stuff," he warned her. "That fool will kill himself someday. You don't have to be party to it and commit suicide too, do you?"

"He's an excellent flier," she said coolly.

"And now what?"

"Dinner," said Judith sweetly, "and I hope you enjoy yours. Good night."

"Good *night!*" said Bill.

She went on into the lounge. Several people stopped her. She had to explain that this was her day off. Candace Howland waved a lazy hand at her from over near the fireplace. And Betty, dashing by with Saks Lewis dogging her high heels, wide round eyes of astonishment. And Bert was waiting for her.

He looked, she admitted to herself, very attractive in the trim mess jacket. And his slow eyes traveling over her from head to foot were assurance that she was easy to look at . . . more than assurance.

"Now where?" she demanded. "I haven't had a day like this since heaven knows when."

"Not my fault," he told her. "You might have given in before. I thought we'd drive out to the Blue Monkey. It's crowded and new and rather fun. There's a floor show of sorts. You'll like it."

It was nearer forty miles than thirty and new territory to Judith. Evidently they were expected. Their table was the best and the orchestra leader sent over to ask what Mr. Wallace would like them to play. Dinner had been ordered by telephone and champagne cooled in a bucket. Judith drank two scant glasses, and watched Bert finish the bottle. She said, "If you think you're going to drive back after all that wine . . ."

"Nonsense!" he said. "I'm perfectly sober."

And so he seemed. They danced between courses and lingered over their coffee, watching the floor show. The place was full of people who had driven over from the nearby summer resorts.

"Like to gamble?" asked Bert softly.

"On life? Of course. No," she amended, considering, "I don't know whether I like it or not really, but I've had to."

"I don't mean on life," he said. "I mean with chips and a roulette wheel."

"Here?" she demanded incredulously.

"Upstairs, in a back room. It's run as a club. All very decorous and well conducted."

She shook her head. "It wouldn't be fun to be caught in a raid. And besides I can't afford it," she said.

"It won't be raided. And I'll stake you."

"Indeed," she said, "you won't. I wouldn't dream of it."

"Mind if I take a turn?"

There was no use arguing. She went with him presently up a staircase which appeared miraculously behind a panel in the manager's office and found herself in a large, quiet, well-filled room. People moved and spoke softly, the click of the ball was the only sharp sound. Judith stood there, mildly interested, thinking with nostalgia of Monte Carlo — her one trip there with Aunt Emily the summer she was sixteen — and watching Bert win some two hundred dollars and then lose it and two hundred more with equal carelessness.

She touched his shoulder.

"It must be very late," she murmured.

He was playing his last stack of chips. When they'd vanished he shook his head, said, "Foolish way to lose money, isn't it? But more fun than most ways," and rose. Presently they were downstairs again and out in the fresh cool air.

He said, standing by the car:

"Seems a pity to go back tonight."

"What do you mean?" she asked him sharply.

"We could so easily have an accident," he suggested, "or run out of gas on a lonely road. The Blue Monkey has very charming little cottages, quite secluded back there in the woods. All the comforts of home including wood-burning fireplaces if the mountain air — or the lady — grows chilly."

She said, "You're being pretty absurd."

"Why?" he demanded. "I can always get you home before dawn. And no one would give that a thought. Lots of eminently respectable people come home before dawn. He went around to the luggage compartment and opened it and produced a suitcase. "I always carry a toothbrush," he said calmly: "ready for any emergency, that's me."

Judith stood perfectly still. She had enjoyed this day. She was young, and escape from routine, any routine, is welcome to youth. Bert had been — nice. He'd said and done nothing offensive till now. Now he stepped to her side, put his arm around her, tilted her face up to his with his free hand. "I think I've earned my kiss," he said.

She suffered it, too appalled to struggle. Then he released her. "Well," he said, "that's better, if not too good. How about it, Judith?"

CHAPTER IX

It was a long way to Hillhigh. Judith had a swift idiotic vision of herself thumbing her way back. The picture was comic — and vulgar. She found her emotions difficult to tabulate. She knew that she was hotly angered, inwardly seething. But to give her rage expression must come later. There wasn't time now. And slapping complacent faces and hissing "Sir, how dare you!" had gone out of style a good many years ago. There were other ways.

"That's a joke, I take it," she said calmly. "Anything for a laugh. Well, it just isn't funny, Bert."

He pulled a pack of cigarettes from his pocket and lit one. She saw his face briefly in the little, ephemerally brilliant flare of the match.

"I'd hate to have you laugh," he informed her, "because it wasn't intended as a gag."

"It would be better — if still not in the best of taste — had you permitted me to believe it was," she told him, walking over to put her hand on the door of the car.

"And it's time we went back to River-mount."

"Okay," he agreed with infuriating cheerfulness. "Any man's entitled to one mistake, isn't he?"

He opened the door for her and presently they had pulled away from the Blue Monkey and were on their way. If he was sullen, if he was ashamed, if he felt anything at all, he concealed it expertly. He talked as if nothing had occurred; gossiped, harmlessly enough, about some of his fellow guests, recounted the news in his last letter from his mother — "She sent her love to you, Judy" — and speculated, not without malice, upon Miss Candace Howland.

"Woman without background. That would make a good title, don't you think? You can't place her somehow. I know people in Washington. So far I haven't hit on a name that means anything to her. She appears to have plenty of money," he added musingly. . . . "Look here, you're pretty quiet."

"Did you expect me to burst into song?" she inquired acidly.

"Oh, come off it," he suggested, with a hint of impatience, "I didn't mean anything, Judy."

"A few minutes ago you assured me that you did!"

"Perhaps I was just experimenting . . . trying to see how serious you were when you told me that maybe — mind you, I accept the reservation — you were gunning for a husband."

"Do you think that a place like the Blue Monkey is the best start for a safari?" she inquired.

"It has been done," he informed her airily.

Judith turned a little, partially facing him. She couldn't see his features clearly in the little light from the dashboard. She asked quietly:

"Bert, hadn't we better get things straight? We've known each other a long time. Five years, four years, even two years ago it would have no more occurred to you to make such a suggestion to me than — Well, I give up," she admitted, helplessly. "If the fact that I no longer live at Carcassonne or on Chestnut Hill, the fact that I am trying to work for my living, could so change the attitude of a man I've known since we were children together . . . it just doesn't make sense. I've read of such things, of course, but they seemed like the wildest flights of imagination to me, with no relation to life at all."

"Listen," said Wallace, without rancor, "you haven't heard my side. Also you haven't grown up and aren't living in this generation. It's no longer a question of being on dining terms with a girl's family and it hasn't anything to do with whether you earn your living or charge things to your parents' accounts. Not any more. It's merely a matter of how two people decide to live their lives. And no questions asked. You told me pretty plainly that you were on your own. You also told me that you were on the make for orange blossoms, slow music and a platinum band. Okay. I wouldn't spoil your fun for anything. Or would I?" he added as if to himself. "The point is, I'm plenty crazy about you. I haven't the slightest desire to, or intention of, marrying you or anyone else. I like things the way they are. Someday I'll marry, I suppose — my old man's forever at me to settle down and find the right girl. Or vice versa. His words anyway." He laughed. "But there's time for that. And here's a grand summer going to waste. If you liked me — and it's apparent that you don't — we could have a swell time together. You're lonely, and so am I — perhaps you're bored too, as bored as I am. And if I'm the first man to suggest a sort of holiday partnership to you I won't be the last, not by a long shot. There'll be plenty who'll size you up for a modern, intelligent girl with plenty of what it takes and who'll ask you up to see their etchings, or water colors or collection of jade, or whatever it happens to be."

She said coolly:

"I've no desire to be added to a jade collection."

"That's pretty neat." He chuckled appreciatively. "Of course not. Not to my collection. Because you don't like me, Judy, any too well. But someday a man will come along whom you will like — what then?"

"Then," answered Judith, "I'll marry him — if I can."

"Suppose he doesn't want to marry you, or can't afford to," asked Bert shrewdly, "or is already married?"

"Why must you assume obstacles?" she asked, interested in spite of herself.

"You'd be astonished how often there are obstacles," he said.

"In that case," she told him, "I'd run away."

"You haven't run away from Bill Martin," he reminded her.

"What in the world has he to do with it?" she demanded.

"Enough, I'm beginning to think. I wasn't sure until a little while ago."

She said, trying to steady her voice:

"Because I'm not interested in your — collection, you assume that I am interested in Bill Martin? That's a pretty clear example of your ego, Bert. I don't want you; therefore, according to your reasoning, I must be in love with someone else. I never heard anything more absurd!"

He ignored that completely.

"Little Betty," he remarked conversationally, "will have your head on a platter when she finds out. And Martin . . . well. I haven't the foggiest notion how he feels but, if he's the wise lad I take him for, he'll avoid permitting himself to grow serious over any delightful but nonsolvent young woman. All things being equal," he added coolly, "Betty's not such a bad bet for him, you know."

"I wish," said Judith, "that you'd talk about something else!"

"Certainly. But I just want to warn you, Judy. You warned me, you know. You even scared me a little. I said to myself, 'Bert, old man, pull yourself up by the bootstraps because if this gal makes up her mind to get you she's apt to be as good as her word.' "

She said scornfully:

"I doubt if you were very frightened, Bert. If you had been you wouldn't have recommended the Blue Monkey hideaway."

"Nonsense," he denied vigorously. "I wasn't making any promises and the Gillmores don't take their problems to court. I know you *that* well anyway. But what I was going to say is this: sometime the man will come along who won't wind up behind the eight ball."

She asked him incredulously:

"Do you mean to tell me that you think all women — ?"

"Most of them, my dear," he interrupted gaily, "most of them. I haven't had much reason to think otherwise. And if you're different, it's because you can't see me." There was faint astonishment in his voice.

She said after a moment, "You are, I think, the vainest man I've ever known. How your vanity must be galled at the moment!"

"It is," he admitted shamelessly, "if that's any consolation to you."

She said thoughtfully:

"I was — furious with you, Bert, awhile ago, I had all the normal reactions: anger at myself that I could have placed myself in such a position; and at you for your crassness and lack of understanding, shame that you could think of me as you did. It's funny, but I'm not angry any more, I'm not even ashamed. I'm a little sorry for you, I think. You're so — *stupid.* Yes, that's it, so entirely without real intelligence, without even animal intuition. And you're right, I haven't liked you very much. I never have. I have even disliked you. But today, up until after dinner, I didn't dislike you. You were pleasant, you were even good company. I thought, If he stays like this the rest of the summer, I won't mind him at all. I may even like him — a little. Now I neither like nor dislike you," she concluded: "so far as I'm concerned, you simply don't exist."

Bert Wallace drew a long breath. She hadn't slapped him. He rather liked women who slapped . . . one could always catch the hand and kiss it. To strike out was at least a sign of emotion. He didn't mind women who lost their tempers . . . they got over anger. But a woman who spoke her mind like this . . . and who meant it! He was shaken with the urge to jam on his brakes, to drag her to him, kiss her, shake her, beat her . . . anything to force some response from her.

He had been perfectly truthful when he

had told her that he was attracted by her. So he had been, in an utterly unimportant fashion. Nor had he actually expected that she would consent to his outrageous proposal. He had been less than half serious when he made it. He'd wanted more than anything to really see her reaction, and it was an oblique way of getting even with her, he believed, for her handing of the cocktails-for-two situation some weeks ago. Had she consented he would have been utterly astonished. But now, with the recollection of her cool-voiced words echoing in his memory, he was more than attracted to her. He hated her, he desired her, he wished to break her will.

He drove on, controlling his fury and the sudden, exciting stimulation of his interest, and said without the slightest sign of resentment:

"Well, you make it pretty clear. Indifference isn't near so hopeful as hatred, so I've heard. If I say I'm sorry you won't believe me. So I won't. But I can promise you that —"

"No," she said, "don't promise anything!"

He achieved a very creditable laugh.

"Then," he said, "like the old song, 'we never speak as we pass by', is that how it's going to be?"

"Don't be absurd, Bert," she said shortly.

"But if I don't 'exist' for you? I feel like the Phantom of the Opera. The Ghost of Hillhigh, or Who Haunted Rivermount! It's uncanny. I shall probably try creeping up on people to see if I'm really invisible, or swinging from the dining room chandeliers."

"I meant you didn't exist for me — as a man."

"Oops! That wasn't very fair, was it? Look, would you rather I left Rivermount and went somewhere else? I will if you say so."

She didn't believe him but she was startled, nevertheless. She answered after a moment:

"Why should it matter to me, Bert? I've nothing to gain by that and everything to lose. I'm not stupid enough to believe you don't *know* what a weapon you hold against me. I know Mr. Corbin likes me. He is even sorry for me," she added a little bitterly. "But what he feels for me isn't of any importance in comparison with the obligation he's under to your father. You can make things very unpleasant for me at the hotel. I suppose if you set your heart on it you could see that I was fired."

He knew, of course, that he held such a weapon. Her admittance was a bit of strategy which he was quick to admire. For it must all but disarm him. If any idea came to him — and doubtless it would in time — he'd be forced to dismiss it. He couldn't make an open confession of failure and rancor and hurt pride. Not that anyone would understand except Judith: but she was the one person to whom he must not admit failure.

"I didn't mind the things you said a moment ago," he told her. "Hell, of course I minded! But that last bit — masterly, wasn't it? — was going just a little too far."

"I'm astonished," she said, "that you can recognize limitations!"

"I wouldn't get you fired even if I could. I find you much too interesting. If I had felt this way about you, say, some years ago — Well, who knows? Let's make a bargain. If we can't be friends, let's be civil enemies, shall we?"

"I don't feel strongly enough," she told him, "to be your enemy. But I can be civil — I hope. Why not?"

"Civilized girl," he murmured. "Too damned civilized!"

He sounded, for the first time, sulky and disgruntled, and Judith burst out laughing.

She couldn't help it. It was all so unlikely. And yet it was perfectly logical. She had never rehearsed the phrases in which she would refuse a gentleman desirous not of becoming her husband, but of becoming her lover — during a holiday. Had she considered such an event she would have found herself forming the conventional, rather melodramatic sentences one associates with such situations. But when it had really happened she had remained — as Bert put it — civilized. Or was she merely cautious? In other circumstances would she not have told him off roundly, smacked his face hard into the bargain and walked home — all forty miles! But those other circumstances lay far behind. In the present set she was forced to be cautious . . . so much depended upon it. But she hadn't been very cautious after all; she had told him exactly what she thought of him, minus adornment or extravagance.

Well, it had been quite a day. She had rescued Aunt Hetty's cat. She had had a very good lunch in pleasant surroundings, her first airplane flight in some time, followed by an excellent dinner. She had parried what was bluntly an attempt at seduction . . . or was foiled a more interesting term? She had tried all day to put

141

Bill Martin out of her mind and had not succeeded, he had been there like an undercurrent, an orchestra accompaniment, an unbidden guest, a dream within a dream. And now she was as tired as if she had done a hard day's work and as drowsy as if she had been listening to Wayne King's soothing melodies beside a fire . . . although she'd made an enemy.

She had. But what she didn't know, and wouldn't know for some time, was that she had made of Bert Wallace the most dangerous enemy of all — for his enmity included something which, for Wallace, passed for love.

They had reached Hillhigh. The village slept, in almost every house the lights were extinguished. Over the drugstore, however, a yellow globe burned and two or three young men were lounging around the street corner in front of it. A belated couple walked up Main Street hand in hand.

At the hotel.

"Thanks," said Judith, "for a very entertaining — and unusual — evening." She suppressed a yawn, and looked at him squarely in the light from the veranda, appearing, he saw with angry resentment, as fresh and lovely as if the evening were just

142

beginning. "How fortunate," she added gently, "that we didn't run out of gas on the way home."

Well, *damn* her! he thought sincerely, watching her walk up the steps and to the big doors. He turned, too impatient to wait for a night boy to drive his car to the garage, took it there himself. The suitcase, which he had tossed back in the luggage compartment, rattled suddenly, like the bones of a forlorn hope.

CHAPTER X

The next morning, at her desk, trying to figure three picnics and a luncheon party, wondering if it was her business to inform little Lily Dawson's mother that she had twice seen the sixteen-year-old child slip out of the hotel with Saks Lewis's pianist, when she should be in bed, Judith looked up to see Bill standing beside her.

"Top of the morning and all that," she said cheerfully, "you're looking very fit."

"It's more than I can say of you," he retorted, staring at her; "you look like something none but a mother could love."

"I was trying to decide something," she said absently. As she spoke she decided it. She'd talk with Saks, Saks could speak to the pianist. The last thing the orchestra leader would want was a scandal centering about one of his band . . . and if she knew anything about Lily's mother, Mrs. Dawson could make more sound and fury than the whole orchestra in jam session.

"Well, have you?"

"I have." She looked at him again, looked away. "I'll admit it," she told him,

"I have the grandfather of all headaches. I feel as if I had been beaten in a dark alley, thumped on the cranium with a couple of marble ninepins. I daren't move my head suddenly. I'm afraid it will split."

"So that's it! Well, come along to my office. I'll be there for half an hour or so, and I'll see if I can't fix you up."

He was off without another word. She didn't want to go to his office. She didn't want to do anything but put her head down on the desk and stay there and not move. But she couldn't. She had work to do. Working girls went on working despite headaches. Hotel hostesses couldn't give in to mere physical discomfort.

"Good morning, Miss Gillmore," said a frosted voice, and a Mrs. Trenter sailed by, leaving the air in refrigeration. Judith looked after her. What on earth had she done? Then she remembered and smiled, resigned. Was it her fault if Trenter, the fat, pompous idiot, couldn't arrange his own golf games and asked her to find him a partner . . . with a willingness to gamble and the proper handicap?

Candace Howland came along looking very smart in her white linen suit and sandals. She was very nearly a beautiful woman, Judith thought, bidding her good morning.

145

Candace came over and sat down beside the desk. Why wasn't she entirely beautiful? Judith wondered, hating to turn her head, hating to smile, to look alert and anxious to help and please. Was it because her features were just a little too classic and controlled, because she had a lacquered, veneered look, a glaze such as one sees on fine porcelain?

"I hate to trouble you," said Miss Howland mendaciously.

"No trouble," Judith assured her, as sincerely. "What can I do for you?"

"It's just that I expect some friends . . . this afternoon. They will be motoring by and wired they might stop by at teatime. It isn't a fixed engagement. I'm going fishing with Mr. Wallace. If we should be late — or delayed —"

Judith knew all about the fishing expedition. Not only had Bert told her on the previous day but she had found his note in her mailbox when she came, a little late to breakfast that morning. It had for no good reason — at least no reason that she'd been able to discover — added to her headache.

"Dear Judy: Off to fish, about ten-thirty. Will you have them put up a lunch for three? Yours, Bert."

146

Well, anyway, he wouldn't get her fired till she'd seen to his lunch! For three: himself, Miss Howland, and the captain he'd hired along with the boat. Miss Howland, she deduced, might not enjoy the presence of a laconic chaperon.

"I see. So, if you aren't back —"

"Oh, I expect we will be. But you know how it is when you go out in a boat." She shrugged and Judith suppressed a desire to inform her that not even Bert's ingenuity could contrive to get them becalmed in a boat without sails and possessing a good steady motor. "If they come, well, will you make them comfortable — see that they get tea or drinks and all that? I'm rather hoping they'll come back here for a stay."

"You haven't told me their names," said Judith.

"Oh, my dear, I'm so sorry! A Mr. Ellerton, and some friends. I don't know their names."

She rose, thanked Judith with a smile and drifted away. Judith thought, Ellerton? Ellerton? Then she sat up suddenly despite the discomfort it caused her. Mrs. Ellerton! The weekend problem child, with a History. The Garbo-divorcée who had lost her husband to a wicked brunette. Now, would one call Miss Howland a wicked brunette?

One might.

Thoughtfully and a little amused, Judith looked at her watch, made two telephone calls from the house phone on her desk, after which she departed, with reluctance, for Bill's office. But she had to go. She couldn't get through the day unless he helped her.

She knocked and was admitted. Bill rose from his desk, apologizing for his shirt sleeves. "It's hotter than blazes," he said, and motioned her to a chair. He then regarded her with, apparently, impersonal and very professional eyes. He asked her a number of questions. One of them was, "Did you have much to drink last night?"

"It isn't that kind of headache," she said angrily; "at least I don't think so as I've never had too much to drink!"

"Well, all right. Calm down. But you will go racketing around at all hours of the night. I — I saw you come in," he said.

Very likely he had. His windows overlooked the side drive, by which she and Wallace had approached the entrance.

"It wasn't late," she said indignantly.

"No, not very. Stomach upset?" he inquired briskly.

"It is not. Must we have a third degree? My head just aches, and that's all there is to it unless I'm coming down with something," she added, with foreboding.

Bill rose and went around behind her. "Relax," he ordered, and she tried, unsuccessfully. She felt his hands on the back of her neck, gentle, impersonal.

"It feels like a poker," she said a little breathlessly.

"Nerve tension," he diagnosed briefly. "I'll fix you up." He vanished into his tiny dispensary and came back with something that foamed in a tall glass. "Drink this," he commanded, "all of it. Then be quiet."

She drank it, and obeyed, her hands folded in her lap. Bill sat down again.

"Tell me about Aunt Hetty and her cat," he said after a little while.

She told him, smiling. "She isn't as bad as she pretends," she said. "She was nice to me. And she dotes on that animal. And you should see her kitchen, it's as scrubbed as scrubbed!"

"Thanks, she doesn't ask me in," he said shortly.

"But she is interested in you, Bill," she hastened to assure him, "she spoke about you. Said she'd seen me with you." She paused, recalling other things Miss Martin had said and found herself flushing, to her great resentment. "And she asked me to be sure not to tell you that she'd even mentioned you," she added hastily.

" 'It's all very well to dissemble your love,' " quoted Bill gloomily, " 'but why must you kick me downstairs?' " Then he laughed. "Poor old girl, I'm sorry for her. But there isn't anything I can do about it. I've tried to unbend her, but she just won't be unbent. I've even given up yelling at her as I go by. How's the head?" he asked abruptly.

"A lot better . . . yes, it really is."

"Can you get off for an hour?" he inquired. "If so, go to your room and lie down. Open the windows —"

"Lord, Bill, they are open and there isn't a breath of air."

"Well, pull down the shades, lie flat, shut your eyes, and rest . . . by luncheon you'll be a new woman."

"I begin to believe you," she said gratefully.

"How'd you get yourself into this nervous state?" he inquired.

"Me, nervous?" she demanded.

"Of course, all tied up in knots." He looked at her, looked away. "Anything unpleasant happen yesterday?" he inquired.

She suppressed a desire to say hysterically, "Oh, no, nothing at all, except that Bert Wallace, my dear old playmate, invited me to spend the night with him at a place called the Blue Monkey. Appropriate name, wasn't it?" Instead, she managed a smile. "No — just as I told you when I saw you before dinner, lunch, a really thrilling airplane hop and after that dinner and home. But the day was, perhaps, a little long."

"Sounds very social," he said, "and that's that. I've got to get along to the hospital now. Sure you'll be all right?"

"I'm fine. Or will be — soon, thanks to you."

"It was nothing," he said, but lingered, staring down at her as if he wanted to say something. But he seemed to think better of it. Judith rose, finding to her amazement that it had ceased to pain her to move, to walk. Her head still ached but not with that malevolent ferocity.

"I think I will go to my room," she said.

"Good girl." He opened the door, and walked to the lounge with her. Near the elevator she was halted by one of the grill-room waiters, a basket in his hands. He said "Excuse me, Miss Gillmore, but Mr. Wallace's lunch — He isn't in his rooms."

151

"Oh, thank you, Fred. I think he's down at the pier," she said. "Yes," she added, "there's Miss Howland, going to join him. If you'll follow her . . ."

"Thanks, miss," said Fred, departing.

"So Bert," mused Bill aloud, "is picnicking with the mysterious Miss Howland. Sure that isn't the cause of your headache?"

Judith looked at him and then turned away. There wasn't any use trying to answer that one. She went on to her own room and pulled down the shades. They would keep out the air but there wasn't any air to keep out. She lay, in dimness, across her bed for some time, and fell finally into a light sleep. When she woke it was noon and as she sat up, a little groggily, she found that her headache had vanished.

Guiltily, she bathed her face in cool water, powdered, brushed her hair and went back to her post. Thank heaven, she was not chaperoning the picnics this morning. No notes were on her desk and no one had telephoned her room or she would have awakened. She sat down, picked up the house phone and asked to be connected with Willow Cottage, where the orchestra men were living.

Saks Lewis answered.

"Saks? This is Judith Gillmore. Would

you mind stopping by my desk on your way in to lunch?"

"Coming right over," he assured her, "just got in from tennis."

Saks, she thought, replacing the instrument, was having a very good time. He wasn't earning much money but he rated board and lodging. And there were plenty of pretty girls. Everyone accepted him and his "nice boys." And they could play. A visiting weekender, connected with one of the New England radio stations, had arranged a hookup Saturday nights from the grillroom. It might lead to something at the end of the season.

Saks came by, cheerful and good-looking in his white flannels, and dropped down in the chair beside her.

"What's on your mind?" he inquired.

"Oh, this and that." She looked around. But her desk was well off the beaten track, no one was writing letters nearby, and at the moment there were few people in the big many-windowed lounge, gay with chintz and flowers.

"I wanted to ask you about your pianist," she said.

"Pete?" He looked astonished. "What about him? He's a good egg."

"Hard-boiled?"

"Oh, a little. Why?" He looked troubled suddenly. "Hasn't been talking out of turn, has he?"

"No, it's the Dawson youngster. She's been going out to meet him after the grillroom dancing is over. And that's late, Saks. She's supposed to be in bed long before. She's only sixteen and as rattle-brained as they come. Her mother's pretty formidable. Money, influence, everything. It so happens that she's a contract fiend, plays till one or two in the morning. She hasn't the remotest idea what the child does. But Lily's been seen, and I was told . . . and I saw her myself. I don't want to speak to her, she'd resent it bitterly; and I won't, of course, say anything to Mrs. Dawson unless I have to. I know she'd pack up and go, and that wouldn't be good for us. Not only would we lose her custom but she would talk about Rivermount at the top of her lungs wherever she happened to be. So I thought the best way out would be to ask you to speak to Pete himself."

"I'll speak to him," muttered Saks, "if it has to be with a brick. He's harmless," he assured her, "and the Dawson kid looks a lot older than sixteen. Pete's a dumb ox, he's probably just flattered and lonesome.

He's got a girl, by the way, back in Maine. A nice one. Don't worry, Miss Gillmore, I'll put a flea in his ear!"

"Good, and tell me how you make out." She smiled at him and he smiled back. "I'm ever so grateful," she said.

"I'm the one to be grateful," he assured her. "You don't know how much this job means to me. If anything happened and we got fired, I'd never get over it," he muttered youthfully.

Judith waited. She saw signs of a confidence coming on. She didn't want to listen but it was part of her unofficial business to listen to confidences.

"Betty," he admitted finally, and with a deep sigh.

"Of course," said Judith, "and she's a darling."

"You're telling me! Not that I stand a chance."

"She's very young, Saks."

"Not too young to be completely gone on Doc Martin," said Saks unhappily. "She just thinks I'm amusing. I give her a good laugh. But with Martin —"

"Nonsense," interrupted Judith. "All youngsters fall in love with their doctors."

"And I," said Saks, "am not what the doctor ordered!" He stopped suddenly, stared at Judith and flushed boyishly. "Gosh," he said, "this time *I'm* talking out of turn!"

Now it was Judith who felt the blood hot in her cheeks. For a moment she had forgotten the half sentence she had overheard from the pergola. So Saks thought she was in love with Bill Martin too! Thought? Knew! And how many other people? And Bill?

She said, trying to recover herself:

"Of course not. I find being a hotel hostess has all the elements of housemother in a boarding school — a coeducational school, I might add. But since you yourself approached the subject, Saks, Mr. Corbin is not very happy over your attentions to Betty."

"He wouldn't be," said Saks. "I'm just a hired hand around here."

"That's not the reason," began Judith, "he —"

"What's disgraceful about leading an orchestra?" he broke in. "I'm going places someday. You watch. Someday I'll have the best band in these United States and I'll make plenty of jack. More than Corbin ever saw in his whole life. There's nothing wrong with that, is there? Or with going to college and deciding that your father's hardware business didn't interest you? My people," he told her, very young and very defiant, "can't afford to spend a season at Rivermount, but they could afford to see me through school. I cannot afford Rivermount either, unless I'm paid to stop here, but someday I'll come and hire the damned place for — for a garage!" he concluded, and then laughed at himself and at Judith's expression. "Now," he said, "I suppose you think I'm just adolescent."

"A little. Have you ever been in love before?" she inquired.

"Who, me? Before Betty, you mean? Oh, dozens of times," he said generously, and added, with alarm, "but not seriously."

"Sure this is serious?"

"How could I help it?" he demanded. "She's the most marvelous, the prettiest . . ." He broke off again and eyed Judith suspiciously.

"You're kidding," he said, with sad finality.

"No."

"I wish you'd put in a word for me," he said; "not that anyone's word would do me any good."

"Mine wouldn't," she admitted ruefully, "even if I were so minded. Betty made quite a confidante of me back in May. But not any more. And I don't," she added, "know why."

"Of course you know why," he burst out. "It's as plain as the nose on your face, which isn't plain at all," he assured her hastily. "She knows that Doc Martin hasn't a dime's worth of time for her when you're around." He said this with open wonder, as if he could not credit Bill's powers of selection.

She didn't color, thank heaven, this time. But she felt as if she paled instead and her fingertips tingled, as fingers do when they have been asleep and the circulation returns. She said, "Look here, Saks, don't you think this is getting rather involved?" and then drew a deep breath. So that was the conclusion of that unfinished sentence. She didn't believe it, she had no evidence but —

Well, what of it, even if it was true? She'd been over that ground before, hadn't she? Where would it get them? Not that she would mind hard sledding, she thought, remembering Aunt Hetty's comment; she'd love it. But it wouldn't be fair to Bill. Too good a doctor, he was, she was sure of that, to tie himself down at the very outset with a wife who wouldn't be able to help him get ahead. I wish I'd trained for a nurse, she thought, hardly listening to Saks' stammering apologies, but smiling at him beatifically, so radiantly that he stuttered into silence and, mentally, found that he couldn't really blame Martin, after all.

She would have made a bad nurse, she concluded, as Saks took himself off; in that capacity she probably wouldn't have met Bill anyway!

Judith went in to lunch, comported herself like a human being, talked with Mr. Corbin, but her mind was certainly not on her work. Betty dashed in late, just as they were finishing. She flung her father a challenging look and said that she had to eat and run, she had a date. She did not deign to say with whom. Mr. Corbin sighed. Betty grew more difficult every day. He had so hoped that Judith would help him with his particular personal problem; had believed so until lately. Betty had taken such a fancy to Judith — at first. But now, it appeared, she had recovered from her childish admiration. Recently she had even said things about Judith — trivial, to be sure, but the reverse of complimentary.

Betty was talking about Candace Howland.

"I think she's keen," she said, glowing,

"and, boy, can she wear clothes! And she's nice too — I mean she goes out of her way to be friendly. Don't you think she's smooth?" she inquired, turning her bright eyes from one to the other.

Judith said, yes, she thought so. Mr. Corbin agreed, with the reservation which was part of his character and also, perhaps, part of his business. Betty, sensing that she was not being met with an enthusiasm equal to her own, shook back her mane of yellow curls. "She's going to ride with me every day," she informed them.

Her father looked thoughtful and Judith's dark brows were briefly drawn. She didn't, she was sure, approve of this new association for Betty but it was certainly not her affair. The mention of Candace reminded her of the expected guests who might not find their hostess waiting for them. In fact, Judith was pretty certain that Candace had no intention of being back at the hotel on time.

Nor was she. An elaborate car rolled up, and a tall lean man, with two other rather nondescript males, presented himself at the desk to inquire for Miss Howland. Following instructions, a clerk said blandly that Miss Howland had left a message for Mr. Ellerton with Miss Gillmore. Miss

Gillmore was duly sought and found, near the tea table which was already set and, coming forward, made Candace's excuses.

"She will be back any moment," reported Judith, hoping that she was not lying. "She's out fishing — and she said to ask if you would not have tea and make yourselves comfortable."

They gazed at her with appreciation. They accepted. In fact, before their cups were empty — and each was astonished to find that he held a cup and not a frosted glass — Mr. Ellerton had decided that there was no sense in pushing on this afternoon, they might as well stop the night if his guests were agreeable.

They were.

Candace trailed in twenty minutes later, with Wallace conspicuously in tow. It was perfectly planned, thought Judith, with admiration. She also thought that Mrs. Ellerton, poor problem child, had probably been mistaken. It did not look to Judith as if Miss Howland had been the one to say no. If so, why this parade of larger game?

Candace met Mr. Ellerton's friends and presented Wallace. She was delighted to learn that dear George and his guests would stop overnight. "I told you this was a charming place," she said.

George agreed, and added, his eyes on Judith, that Candace hadn't said the half of it. Tea being over, Judith rose to slip away, to see that the accommodations for the newcomers could be arranged. But Mr. Ellerton, muttering something about speaking to the manager, followed and caught up with her near the desk. She was beginning to be adamant to astonishment, hence it was with a sense of familiarity that she heard him say, jovially, this lean man with the weak mouth and roving eyes, "Suppose I come back, say, next week? I like this place. I might be induced to take myself a vacation if you'd be nice to me."

She wasn't the only one who heard. Candace and Bert, following hard on their heels, heard too.

CHAPTER XI

Judith felt rather than saw Bert Wallace's slow smile. He promptly engaged the amiable Ellerton in conversation as an instant later they turned away from the desk. "By the way, Mr. Ellerton," he asked, "are you by any chance a collector?"

"Collector?" inquired Mr. Ellerton, astonished. "What do you mean, collector?"

"Oh, first editions," explained Bert casually, "victrola records, match covers —"

"I liked stamps," replied Ellerton, "when I was a kid. Never been able to understand adults who go goofy over a bit of cracked old glass or a hunk of pewter, myself."

"I see," said Bert gravely, "that the fever hasn't caught up with you. Me, I dote on beer-bottle caps."

Ellerton looked at him as if he thought him slightly insane and Judith thought, seized with a wild desire to laugh, "I wish I'd smacked him last night — hard!"

But Ellerton was now devoting himself to her. Wouldn't she dine with them that evening, in the grillroom? His eyes asked, How come a pretty girl like you has to take a job like this? But it's a break for me, isn't it?

"Yes, do," supplemented Candace cordially; and turning to Wallace, "you too," she urged, "let's make a party of it. It's always becoming to a couple of lone women to be surrounded by twice their number of males."

Bert said he'd be delighted. But they must all have cocktails with him before dinner, in his rooms. Judith hesitated appreciably before she accepted. However, if dining in company with Mr. Ellerton and his friends constituted being "nice" and would win him as a guest of the hotel, she didn't mind — much, she told herself. But she would far rather have dined alone, in her room. She had a good deal to think about.

Candace had a moment with her, as the group dispersed.

"You made quite a hit with George," she commented. Her charming smile was bland but Judith received the immediate and strong impression that if the elegant Miss Howland could have cut her throat then and there and got away with it she, Judith, would find herself in a most uncomfortable situation.

She said lightly:

"I imagine that Mr. Ellerton is merely being — pleasant."

She hoped she spoke the truth.

Cocktails in Bert's rooms were, as one might expect, good, strong and served with all the trimmings of appetizers, smoke, laughter and noisy chatter. His non-descript guests turned out to be rather surprising personalities, once Judith had their names straight and learned a little about them. One was, of all things, an expert on the molecular theory and the other was a passionate amateur golfer, and a good one . . . runner-up in the last open tournament. Ellerton himself, she gathered from his gloomy predictions touching on Big Business, was a broker.

It wasn't a very common name. She wondered if there were a Mrs. Ellerton? It was the molecular-theory gentleman who enlightened her by breaking in on his host's glum soliloquy by remarking:

"After all, George, it isn't the high cost of living but the upkeep in alimony that really hurts."

"Marie," said Ellerton with a sorry grin, "was always an expensive proposition."

Judith set down her glass. Marie Ellerton. Yes, that was her problem child, registered on the books as Mrs. Brainley

Ellerton. "But do call me Marie," she had sighed.

Dinner was lavish, and likewise noisy and gay. The grill, in which Judith had not dined this season, achieved an intimate atmosphere without sacrificing space and light and air. Saks Lewis smiled at her as she danced by with the molecular-theory person, who proved an excellent dancer. The orchestra leader's nod and slight shrug were, she assumed, intended to convey to her that he had spoken to his philandering pianist. She stole a look at Pete, sitting hunched over the keyboard. He did look rather down. And when the choice for a number fell on a slow, sentimental waltz or a piece with plenty of Schmaltz in it Pete appeared to give it his all. Little Lily was not to be seen in the grill although of late she had managed to persuade her mother to dine there rather often, despite the old adage, "American plan, eat as much as you can."

The golfer was not at his best on a dance floor. He held Judith in a determined but impersonal clutch, and trod all over her feet. She felt like asking him to replace the divots. Bert, of course, was another matter; Bert held her too close and said very little, simply smiled at her now and then in a most infuriating manner. And Mr. Ellerton, the downtrodden broker, late husband of the problem child, was a problem in himself. He held her even closer than Bert and shouted loud nothings in her outraged ear above the crash of the music.

"Never thought I'd really want to spend a week or two at a summer resort," he bellowed; "like a hunting lodge myself, good fishing and no women rocking on the porch. But a girl like you certainly changes a man's point of view."

She wished he would change his dancing technique.

Oh, well, all in the life of a hostess, she thought much later when she was ready for bed. She had excused herself from the party as soon as possible, in order to run a bingo game for those guests who wished to amuse themselves after that fashion in the larger cardroom. She had been very glad of the legitimate opportunity to get away.

Now, regarding with rancor a run in a new pair of stockings, and experimenting gingerly with her tired toes by a species of tentative exercises, she decided that this was no sinecure; a hostess earned her money and her board and her lodging no matter what anyone said!

On the following day the Ellerton party

went on their way and Candace, stopping Judith in a corridor, said blithely, "George tells me he's thinking of returning. Awfully nice. I've written him a dozen times since I've come here how charming it is. But seeing is believing in his case, and Mr. Corbin is certainly fortunate in having you," she added sweetly, "you're so persuasive."

Harmless word but it sounded like an insult. But, though Judith, entertained, she isn't any too annoyed at having dear George return. Two strings to her bow . . . and a string to her beau, if I must make a pun. If it's George she's after, she can use Bert for bait. Or is the bait bigger than the fish? Like fishing for perch with a pike!

The next day, Wednesday, one of the youngsters, Marise Milton — a fat blond child with all the brutal qualities of Fanny Brice's Baby Snooks and none of her appeal to the risibilities, developed a toothache. Mrs. Milton was playing in a golf tournament, so would dear sweet kind agreeable Miss Gillmore escort darling Marise to the dentist in Valleytown and stay with her? Marise was so timid. If Miss Gillmore would just reassure her and hold her hand?

Miss Gillmore would and did.

Mr. Corbin lent her his car and Betty decided to come along and drive . . . for which Judith was duly grateful; not that she couldn't drive herself, and expertly, but she had dreaded keeping one eye on the road and the other on Marise, who had evidently been born with ants in her small lace-trimmed unmentionables, for she was a twister, a turner and a wiggler of the front rank.

Thinking of the Valleytown dentist made Judith remember the tooth-pulling at which she had assisted Bill during the early days of their acquaintance. How brief a time had passed since then, how long it seemed. She smiled, remembering. Betty, driving well if a little too fast, inquired, "A penny for your thoughts, or are they worth more?"

"A dollar at present rates," answered Judith lightly. Marise sat between them on the front seat of the small car and clamored loudly to ride alone in the rumble. When Judith told her she couldn't she replied. "Yah, sez you," and attempted to climb over. The rumble was open, filled with packages which Judith was taking to the Valleytown post office for one of the guests . . . "If you don't mind, dear Miss Gillmore," said the lady, on overhearing Judith's plans, "they will go out so much faster." She was a visiting novelist, whose annual book had just appeared and she was inflicting copies on her weary friends. A large lady with a massive bosom, she wrote improving novels with an uplift trend.

Arriving in ample time at Valleytown, they went first to the post office where Judith, making trips to and from the rumble, managed to mail all twelve copies safely; and then on to the dentist with Marise growing more recalcitrant every moment. If I were the dentist, thought Judith grimly, I'd yank out every tooth in her empty little head. But she was forced to beam upon the child and coax and plead. Betty wasn't much help. She was bored. And even when Judith said, despairingly and sotto voce, "I wish I had a carrot to dangle before her nose," Betty was not amused.

At the dentist's as they were getting out, or more accurately as Judith was dragging Marise, howling, from the car, wondering wildly if passers-by would think the child was being kidnaped, Betty said suddenly:

"You'll be here half an hour or so, I suppose. Guess I'll run up to the hospital and see Bill. He should be finished there by now."

She stepped on the gas and departed. Judith was left on the sidewalk with her charming charge, feeling faintly in sympathy with King Herod. An old lady passed by and looked at her, with a frown. Another, still older, stopped to inquire, "What *is* the matter with your sweet little girl?" Whereupon Marise, looking like a tub of butter in a maize-colored frock, howled afresh and remarked, "She ain't my mother and I wisht she was dead." Which somewhat startled the sympathetic interlocutor.

At last Judith got her upstairs to the office. She carried her there and Marise retaliated by kicking her, with evil effect. The dentist, however, proved to be a large man with an impressive scowl and a still more impressive smile, and perfectly accustomed to handling children. He took Marise away from Judith in one vast, expert gesture. He said, "I'll manage." And he did.

Judith, savagely determined to keep her promise, held Marise's unappetizing hand while the tooth was prepared for a filling and then filled. Later she staggered out with the slightly subdued child, feeling as if she had been let loose in Chaos. Those appalling shrieks! She hoped that the dentist would charge Mrs. Milton a fortune.

Arrived on the sidewalk she saw that Betty had not returned. Marise was demanding ice-cream cones and lollipops as a sop to her physical discomfort when the Corbin car slid to a stop at the curb. Betty, looking much more animated than when Judith had last seen her, was apologetic. She was so sorry, but she got talking to Bill . . . he let her go up to the nursery and look through the glass at the babies. She'd never seen anything so precious!

Flushed, happy, eighteen; happy because she had been near her idol, because he had spoken to her gently, because she had had him all to herself — in the midst of at least a hundred people — for a moment. Judith was very much afraid that she knew exactly how Betty felt even if she hadn't been eighteen for some years.

She herself saw little of Bill as the days went on. There was a good deal of sickness in the Valleytown section: summer colds, pneumonia, and the following week the start of an infantile paralysis scare. Several anxious mothers at Rivermount, despite the miles between them and the town, packed up their children and left for another part of the country. There was one close call from drowning when, during a regatta, a small boat overturned; and one broken leg, caused by a fat lady near-sightedly stepping off the last step of the veranda, a step which wasn't there. There were the usual minor complaints among the guests, and in Hillhigh itself a perfect epidemic of new babies.

When the week passed and Ellerton did not return, Judith breathed a sigh of relief. And somehow, as though by a tacit understanding, she found that Bill had at least time to take her to lunch on her next Monday off and to come for her again, at the Parsons'. Passing Aunt Hetty's, they saw the old lady raking a flower bed in her yard. Judith waved and Aunt Hetty flapped a dirty hand in her direction, a response which said quite plainly, "I mean this for you and not for him."

"Still adamant," said Bill.

"I went around today," confessed Judith, "before you came for me. And had another ginger cookie. She's a lonely old woman, Bill."

"Well, what can I do about her?" he demanded. "Golly, I'd move in bag and baggage if she'd let me."

"You *would?*"

"Sure. That is, if she'd stand for me coming in and out all hours of the day and night. I don't expect she would. But I wouldn't be much trouble, I could eat at the hotel, as I do now, or get my meals anywhere. It's just," he explained, a little abashed, "that you sort of want someone of your own, no matter how — how uncongenial they may be."

Judith resisted the temptation to put her hand over his as it lay on the wheel. She was very much on her guard with Bill these days. She felt shy with him, almost awkward. Saks' diagnosis of Bill's personal cardiac case had probably been in error, born of his jealousy of Bill and Betty. Yet if Saks was right, the first move must come from him. But he said nothing, he maintained the same friendly, rather teasing attitude toward her. Now and then they quarreled over nothing at all, but wholeheartedly, as if they enjoyed it. They laughed a good deal; and talked. She knew, she thought, more about Bill Martin and his years at the orphanage, his semesters at the university and medical school and his internship than anyone in the world. And in return he learned something of her, of her life, as it had been lived once upon a time, and of her people.

She said, "Look, there's time, isn't there? Let's drive by Carcassonne."

Obediently he swung the car around the

corner, up the street, over the hill along the country road until they reached the gate of the place which was now Bellevue. What a name, she thought. But it was appropriate enough, for the old white house commanded a magnificent vista of mountains, valley and river. It had a great deal of road frontage so they could drive slowly around and look. She could see over the wall that the informal gardens her father had so loved had been replaced with very landscaped formal beds and borders. But the house looked the same.

"Miss it a lot?" he asked gently.

"Terribly. Wish I hadn't come. I've managed to keep away from it up till now, even in my walks."

"You should have it back again."

"You never get anything back, not really."

"Well, then you should have something like it." He glanced at her swiftly. "A substitute. A place you can take and make into a second Carcassonne."

"Don't worry," she said, "I never shall. And it's something to have enjoyed it all those years."

They were passing the Wallace property. The wrought-iron gates were closed and locked. NO TRESPASSING warnings were displayed in great profusion. The big gray-

175

stone house was shuttered and boarded. It looked desolate despite the tended lawns.

"Wallace could give you this," muttered Bill, gesturing.

"I suppose he could," said Judith evenly, but her heart jerked in her breast. "But he doesn't want to. And even if he did, I wouldn't want it."

"The more fool you, then," said Bill firmly, and her heart quieted and grew cold. She did not answer. After all, if he could say that and mean it he couldn't possibly care for her. She looked at him briefly. He must mean it, his face was so still and grave.

CHAPTER XII

Within the next few days George Ellerton returned. He had not been established at Rivermount for more than two hours when Judith saw that she would have her hands full. Luckily the height of the summer season would provide her with considerable occupation. Boat races, fishing parties, golf, badminton and tennis aments, and swimming meets. Picnics and moonlight excursions, dancing and movies, and children's parties. She had a finger in almost every social pie. Guests coming and going and the usual quota of lonely hearts, both male and female, who must be looked after and amused. And the usual influx of old ladies and elderly widows who could be counted on to institute sudden feuds. She stopped taking her day off, despite Mr. Corbin's expostulations, or at least to spend it behind locked doors in her own room, doing the necessary odd jobs which must not be neglected. A spot of manicuring, a shampoo, letters to her mother and her friends, and dinner in bed with a book which she had borrowed from the hotel library. But Bert

Wallace was very much in evidence as Monday neared . . . where would they go, what did she want to do? And Ellerton, having learned somehow, from Betty probably, never Candace or Wallace, that one day a week the hostess was free to be a guest, plagued her interminably.

She finally went driving with him one Monday afternoon and returned stormy and disheveled to the hotel. The man was an idiot, she told herself, and she certainly hadn't been hired by Mr. Corbin to indulge in a sort of catch-as-catch-can with his male guests. Bert, sitting on the veranda, saw her get out of Ellerton's car alone and hurry toward the lounge. He followed and caught up with her at the elevators.

"Not so fast."

"Oh, let me go," she said irritably, shaking his hand from her arm with annoyance. For the moment, so far as she was concerned, all boy babies should have been drowned at birth.

"You look like one of the prettier Furies," he remarked calmly; "better come quietly and cool off and tell Uncle Bert all about it."

He whisked her past the elevators, through the lounge and out to the more secluded part of the veranda. Tea was being served in the lounge, the housekeeper substituting for Judith, and most of the guests who happened to be about were there.

Out on the veranda, overlooking the river, "Well?" he asked.

She said angrily:

"It's really none of your business, but if you must know, George Ellerton should have been born in — in Turkey or someplace."

"Like me to speak to him?" he inquired.

"Of course not," she said, "why should you? And what in the world would he think?"

"I might remind him that I have known you for a good many years and — how is it that they put it so prettily in the movies? — that you are not That Kind of girl. I might even go so far as to say that I'd proof — or perhaps I'd better not," he added hastily as she turned toward him with an upblaze of anger. "In any case, I could say *something*. Unless this is the way you play your lone-wolf hand, Judy, and are just sore because you haven't brought Ellerton to time. He's eligible enough, isn't he?"

Judith looked away toward the mountains and the river. Silly, in the face of the steadfast calm of one and the unhurrying journey of the other toward the sea, to feel so upset and filled with loathing for the human race in general, Ellerton, as an example of it, in particular. Nothing mattered much, really, did it? You just kept on and preserved your own personal integrity as best you could.

She said, more mildly, ignoring his last sentence:

"Thanks, Bert, I know you mean well enough —"

"What a horrible thing to say of anyone!" he exclaimed.

She smiled at him, turned from the veranda railing and walked toward the doors. "I think I'll go to my room now," she said.

"Look. Have dinner with me? I'll behave," he promised.

Judith shook her head. "Sorry, I don't feel like it. I'm cross," she admitted, "and getting crosser all the time. This is one time when solitude is indicated."

Bert watched her go in, shook his head and went in search of Ellerton. He looked at his watch as he went. Betty and Candace were riding, they would be back soon. He had a date with Candace. He yawned. She did not wear very well and she was exceptionally — eager. Well, he was a lot smarter than she, he thought. He could see through her transparent stratagem of playing him against Ellerton. It was funny when you came to think of it . . . Candace outwardly cool but anxious under her poise, determined to make the summer pay. Himself and Ellerton both fully aware of her design for living and each of them determined to make his own design . . . which didn't include Miss Howland.

He strolled on, smiling. He thought that he knew the right approach to Ellerton. It should work. And he believed that Judith would be grateful to him — so long as she didn't know exactly what device he used to free her of dear George.

Judith was grateful to him, for from that day forward Mr. Ellerton was no longer her problem. He devoted himself to Candace. For at least he knew where he stood with Candace, but the Gillmore girl was another matter. "Watch your step, old man," Bert Wallace had warned him pleasantly, "unless you crave to find yourself married before the season's over. Judy's a sweet kid, but this job of hers is just marking time. After all, a girl who's had everything once couldn't be satisfied with this, could she? And if you don't believe me, ask her."

"Ask her?"

"Sure. One of her more brilliant dodges is a disarming frankness. Why, she even warned me when I first came up. Of course, we're old friends but —"

Mr. Ellerton had no intention of marrying again. Marie was, as he had once stated, an expensive proposition. And Candace was — or had been — expensive too. He had bought her off, a neat payment in full, rather than figure in it breach of promise suit. Candace had feathered her nest once before after that attractive fashion. He couldn't for the life of him understand how he had managed to escape her . . . and how she had managed to remain, well, at least his friend. But so it had been. She had conducted the whole affair with a delightful disregard of reality. She had never really threatened in so many words. And she had given him his letters without a struggle. She hadn't asked for payment. But just a little later she had found herself hard up and wrote him asking for a "loan," just to tide her over. That's how it had all happened. No harsh words on either side. And she had continued to write him, as a friend, with a wistful note underlying her light phrases. She must have read a book, he thought gloomily. And somehow he'd found himself committed to stop by Rivermount and see how she was getting along — on his money. And stopping, had seen Judith and, so, had returned. He hadn't believed that Candace would put anything in his way. They were all washed up and he had paid for her summer's hunting.

But Judith was a different matter, with her background and — and everything. Also the afternoon's entertainment, the quiet drive into the country, had amply proved that Miss Gillmore was not interested in the pleasant pastime of holiday dalliance.

He was grateful to Bert too.

And left, within a day or so, because of the sudden pressure of business.

"You had a hand in that," Judith accused Bert, and he just grinned amiably.

"Sorry?" he said.

"Of course not. I'm enchanted. And with the season as it is one more or less doesn't hurt the hotel."

But Candace was puzzled. Mr. Ellerton had given her no explanation for his abrupt decision to return to the city, during the summer heat. She regarded Judith now and then speculatively. But her speculations got her nowhere. She found that an attempted closer friendship with Judith came to nothing also. And it was more amusing to devote herself to little Betty who obviously admired and adored her and who had all the hotel gossip at her pretty, childish fingertips.

Candace knew by now all about Betty's devotion to Bill Martin. She knew about Saks Lewis's hopeless devotion to her. There was nothing that Candace didn't know . . . except what had happened to Ellerton and how matters stood between Judith and Bert Wallace. She would have given her pretty eyeteeth to know that. Bert was her game — now. She had realized before Ellerton had been at the hotel for a day that there was no use raking over dead embers. All you did was soil your hands. And Bert was younger, he had much more money, he was better looking, he had no ex-wife to whom he was forced to pay alimony.

She had tried all her little tricks on Mr. Wallace. So far they hadn't worked. She had "sprained" her ankle slightly when walking with him. She had taken to her bed with a headache and sent for him. . . . "Would you bring me a book? It would be angelic of you." She had endured fishing trips which she hated, she had gone motoring — but Wallace's motor never seemed to run out of gas. It was all very unfortunate.

Bert's vacation drew to a close but he decided that the business could get along without him until after Labor Day. Candace felt as if the decision had given her a respite and hope. She had, she told him, just about decided not to return to Washington at once. New York was so lovely in the autumn. She might take a little flat for the autumn months . . . she had so many friends in Manhattan. It would be exciting, a change. Summer might end and the resort season come to a close but Miss Howland was determined not to abandon her big-game expedition.

"You needn't think you're escaping me too," Bert told Judith, during the Labor Day dance.

"How do you mean?" she asked, smiling. She was no longer very angry with Bert. He had made a nuisance of himself early in the season but after that his conduct, while occasionally infuriating, had been impeccable.

"You've never gone for another hop," he said.

"I've been so busy."

"Even Mondays? Well, I'm flying back weekends. And I'm a keen skier . . . you didn't know that, did you? So when the snow falls, I'll be falling with it . . . for you," he added softly.

185

"Bert, must you be so absurd? You sound like a popular song."

"Without music. It will be nicer in winter anyway. Fewer people — you'll have time on your hands."

"You won't be able to fly up," she reminded him.

"There'll be fast trains."

"When are your mother and father coming home?" she asked.

"Not till spring or later. They're going to England to visit Edith and that dime-a-dozen husband of hers. You mean, I suppose, what will my father say when he discovers that I've neglected business for — what might be pleasure? Well, he won't say anything. He's always doubted me as a businessman. Yet I haven't done so badly, you know. I made some good clients for the firm this summer and you'd be surprised how much can be accomplished over a toddy of spiced wine after a day's skiing. I'm not so dumb as you think, my dear."

He had been rather clever, he thought, during the past weeks. He hadn't alarmed her. He hadn't even angered her, very much. He could afford to be patient. At first he had believed that Bill Martin was the real obstacle. But there had been no evidence to prove that theory. Sooner or later, he thought, now that she is off her guard . . .

He could not endure opposition to his will. He had broken the will — and the spirit as well — of half a dozen good dogs in his day. He had done the same with his horses. He could not endure that anything should defy him. Least of all this red-headed black-eyed girl whom he had known for most of her life.

So he would wait.

After Labor Day the season was over. The vacationists went home and presently the hotel was half empty again. But enough remained, the elderly, the idle, the convalescents, to keep Judith busy. In fact, she was almost busier then than at the season's height, for less things were planned to amuse the guests.

Saks Lewis and his boys departed also. They had procured an engagement in Boston, at one of the hotels. Saks, after the last dance, took Betty away from everyone, out of the hotel, onto the grounds.

She sat there beside him in their regular meeting place, the old pergola, close, yet a hundred miles away.

"Will you miss me, Betty?"

"Of course."

"I don't believe it. You're crazy to get rid of me. Crazy to have the people go — so you can see more of Martin."

"Well, what if it's true?" she demanded.

"I wish it weren't. You won't give me another thought." He was sunk in gloom, despairing as only the young can despair.

"Of course I will. And I'll come to Boston — Marge Higgins has asked me to visit her this autumn — so I'll see you, Saks. And I'll write."

"Every day?"

"Silly, of course not, what would there be to say?"

"If you loved me," he told her, "you'd find plenty."

"Please, Saks."

But he had clutched her and now held her despite her halfhearted struggles, kissing her eyelids, her childish cheeks and her young mouth. "I do love you so much."

If it hadn't been for Bill, she thought, not especially dismayed and not in the least repulsed, she might have loved Saks. He was sweet, really, and so crazy about her.

Well, the season was over. Judith was tired, to her marrow. Mr. Corbin had very kindly suggested a little vacation. But where would she go? Chicago was too far and, besides, she couldn't afford it. So she shook her head and told him that she wasn't tired at all, that they all would have plenty of time to rest now that there wasn't so much going on.

"But there will be," he said, "weekends specially. We'll have a hunting crowd up first thing you know. And everyone prophesies an early winter. In which case we'll have the skiers up in full force before you can say Telemark."

On Mondays she went again to the village, to see the Parsons and Mr. Alcot, and always stopped by to have a cookie with Aunt Hetty and pretended that she didn't know the old lady was pumping her about Bill. "What's that good-for-nothing of a Bill Martin been up to?" Aunt Hetty would ask slyly, as if she believed that Judith didn't know what she was after. And Judith would tell her — long stories of hard work and healing. Sometimes she made things up. She confessed as much to Bill, laughing. "Someday you're coming in with me," she said, "and ask her, 'Aunt Hetty, may I have a cookie too?' "

"Not me," denied Bill. "Once bitten twice shy. It's a wonder she didn't give me hydrophobia the first time I tried barging in, guileless as a child, back last spring."

"You're as stubborn as she is," Judith accused him.

"I waved at her for quite a spell."

"That," diagnosed Judith, "was out of meanness!"

They were still, it appeared, on their old friendly footing, right where they had been at the beginning. Saks was a notional kid, imagining things, she thought hopelessly.

She hadn't liked Candace but she rather missed her, and all the excitement. But there wouldn't be any excitement until it snowed, she thought one windy blue October morning, walking down to the river before luncheon. A man whom she recognized as one of the gardeners came stumbling up to meet her. He was a ghastly color, a dirty green. He said, gasping, "A man — shot himself — down there."

Judith began to run. She called back, "Get Dr. Martin, at once. *Hurry.*"

The man was lying under the trees near the river. She reached him, fell on her knees beside him, staring incredulously at the horror and the blood. She knew him despite the mutilation. He was Mr. Carlin, a hotel guest, a quiet man who had come up a few days ago. He had exacted nothing of anyone, he was a gray, strange man. She stared at him, sick and shaken. Bearded, his eyes closed. She thought, But I *do* know him. I've seen him before . . . I didn't realize it until now.

Bill came galloping down the terrace, cutting across the lawns. "For God's sake, Judith!" he cried.

She turned, rose and tried to stand.

"I know him," she said, as if astonished, "he didn't have a beard then . . . that's the man . . . that my father . . . I mean . . . he's been in prison, you know . . . and now . . ."

She swayed toward him and he caught her as she fell.

"Judith," he said, completely unprofessional for a split second. "Judith, my darling."

She was unconscious. She did not hear his words nor feel his kiss. But Betty, riding her little mare along the river bridle path and coming upon them suddenly, heard and saw.

CHAPTER XIII

Other people, led by the gardener who had found Mr. Carlin's body, came running across the grounds. Betty dismounted and cut across to join the group. She found Judith struggling back to consciousness and Bill busy with the man on the ground. But Betty was not interested in the accident — if it was an accident — to the hotel guest. She had seen the expression on Bill's face, she had heard his voice. It was enough.

Her father, summoned from his office, was waving her away. He called, "Go back, Betty, you can't do any good here . . . and you too, Judith," he added, turning, seeing her stand finally, wavering a little, her hand against a tree trunk.

Bill rose from his knees. He said briefly to Mr. Corbin, "It's a case for the coroner. He died — instantly — suicide, of course."

Judith exclaimed, brokenly, and put the back of her hand across her mouth. The tears were running down her cheeks. "It was my fault," she managed to say.

Corbin went to her and put his arm around her. "You go back to the house with Betty. Please, my dear."

"You don't understand," she said a little wildly. "His name isn't Carlin at all. It's Benner . . . Frederick Benner. I didn't recognize him when he came here, he's altered so, he's lost so much weight . . . and he used to be clean-shaven. I didn't even recognize his voice, for to the best of my knowledge he never spoke to me. He knew me, of course, as soon as he set eyes on me. He — Benner — was my father's friend, Mr. Corbin . . . the one who took the money. He's been in prison . . ."

"Come back with us," said Corbin soothingly, "I'll have to telephone the police. This is a dreadful thing to have happened." He looked at Judith anxiously. "We'll try our best to keep you out of it."

Much later, when the coroner had come and gone, when they had removed the body and notified Benner's people — he had a sister and brother, his wife having divorced him at the time of the trial — Bill knocked on Judith's door.

"May I come in?" he asked.

"Please do," she answered him, sitting up in bed.

"Still feeling rocky?" he inquired.

"Shaky. Recognizing him was the worst, I dare say. I don't know how I did. But there was just something. And I remembered when I first saw him in the hotel that he did look vaguely familiar. I was wrong when I told Mr. Corbin that he hadn't spoken to me. He had — for a moment. It was the first night after he came and I asked him if there was anything I could do for him. He said no, and thanked me and went off."

"We've found out about him," Bill told her, sitting down in the chair by the window. "Mr. Corbin's been in touch with the authorities. Benner was released from prison, on probation, some months ago. Long enough to grow a beard anyway," he added. "No one seems to know how he happened to come here."

"He's been here," said Judith, "a great many times. To Carcassonne. That's what brought him back. Thinking, remembering. He was fond of my father," she added miserably, "and when Father killed himself, he must have suffered agonies. Then getting out of jail and coming back here, driven by some morbid compulsion, seeing Hillhigh again, perhaps, walking past Carcassonne, and remembering the way things used to be. And seeing me . . . That's why he killed himself, and as much as I've blamed him and hated him . . . you don't know *how* bitter I have felt about it, Bill — I blame myself now for his death."

"Don't be sentimental," said Bill shortly, "it was probably the best way out for the poor devil." He rose and stood over her. "Did you take the sedative I sent you?" he inquired sternly. "And did you have lunch?"

"Yes, I took it. I'm all right. Just as I said, shaky. Silly of me. I'm afraid to sleep because I'm sure I'll have nightmares. But I don't want to eat again — ever."

He was too wise to argue with her. He said, "Well, you're going away. Tomorrow. Bright and early, so I'd advise you to sleep if you can. I'll leave you something that will insure a night's rest for you."

"Going away?" she gasped, and her black eyes were frightened, seeking his, "What — What — ?"

"Don't worry," he reassured her. "Mr. Corbin's orders. Mine too. You won't want to see Benner's sister and brother, will you?"

"I know them quite well," she told him, very pale. "But I'd rather not see them. Oh, Bill, don't think me a coward."

"It's the last thought I'd have about you," he said. "Mr. Corbin and I felt you wouldn't want to see them either. They'll be here as soon as they can. Then there are reporters, of course. They're here now. Sooner or later they'll dig you up, in connection with this. Sooner, I dare say, as it would be a perfectly simple routine matter. Benner, alias Carlin, once financial adviser to your father, let off his long term for good behavior. And you here. Everyone knows you, Judith. So the idea is, you're to stay quietly in your room until very early tomorrow morning when you will take Betty to Boston on a little trip. You'll both stay with her friend Marge — what's her name — Higgins, isn't it? Mr. Corbin has talked to Mrs. Higgins by telephone. You'll shop and go to the theater and the movies and — and when you come back there won't be anything to remind you of this. We'll do all we can for Benner's people and we'll take care of the reporters."

"You're both awfully good," she murmured, "and I'm so ashamed of myself . . . passing out like that. What a fool you must have thought me!"

"I didn't care too much about it myself," he said shortly, "and I've seen death by violence more times than I care to count." He rose and came over to the bed. With an awkwardly gentle gesture he pushed the heavy red hair from her forehead. "Well, okay, old-timer," he said, "I'm going to send you in something to eat after a while and you're to eat it. And take the medicine I send. Betty will be in before you go to sleep."

Betty came, shortly after dinnertime. She was rather pale and very subdued. She spoke without enthusiasm of the proposed trip. "You liked Marge, didn't you, when she was here?" she asked.

"Ever so much."

"Well," Betty rose and fidgeted with her handkerchief, "I'll let you get some sleep and if you're sure I can't help you pack. Father will drive us over to the early train."

She lingered as if she wanted to say something more, hesitated, asked with elaborate casualness, "Bill come in to see you?"

"Yes," said Judith and could not for the life of her keep the color from rising. "He scolded me, sent me some medicine."

Betty had, it appeared, lost interest. She went to the door. "Well, good night," she said listlessly.

What in the world was wrong with her? Judith was, of course, aware that Betty's first youthful affection for her had waned. She believed she knew why. It couldn't be helped, no matter how wrong Betty was in her conjecture. But the child seemed so altered this evening. Probably the shock, and the excitement . . . and she must have seen something of the horror, decided Judith, shuddering. She put her hands over her eyes. If only she could forget it. But she was afraid that she would not for as long as she lived.

She did not see Bill before she left for Boston, but she wrote him a little note of thanks, and left it in his box. "Better go see Aunt Hetty," she advised, "she may miss me! You can tell her why I've gone away."

Boston was at its best in the crisp October weather, blue and gold. The Higgins house was big and old-fashioned and comfortable. Marge was delighted to see Betty and Mrs. Higgins, a very pretty woman of not much more than twice her daughter's age, welcomed Judith warmly and would not hear of gratitude.

"Marge has been pining for Betty," she said. "You know how youngsters are their first autumn out of school. They have their longed-for freedom but don't know quite what to do with it. It looks, however, like a busy time ahead — with the football season and the debutante parties. I'm at my wits' end about Marge. She considers herself the menace type, you know, and wants to make her debut in black velvet!"

She and Marge's big, attractive father planned varied entertainment for their guests: pleasant drives out along the deserted beaches with the white foam edging blue water and eating at the rocky ragged coast line; a trip to Cambridge and tea in the rooms of Marge's brother, a Harvard senior, matinees and evening theater, and supper at the hotel where Saks was playing.

He was enchanted to see them, but Judith couldn't believe that he was as astonished as he seemed. Surely Betty had sent him word? But if she had, he was discreet and did not mention it. He maintained, perfectly, the fancy-seeing-you-here pose. And Betty, when he came over to their table between dances, turned immediately from a rather quiet, almost remote eighteen-year-old with all the conscious earmarks of a secret sorrow to a casual and sparkling woman of the world. Mrs. Higgins watched with much amusement. "Isn't it marvelous," she whispered to Judith, "the way the kids manage to treat their devoted swains — for Marge tells me he's very devoted — as long as they don't happen to care anything about them?" She sighed.

"Betty's a darling," she added. "I have my eye on her for Roger. And you may have noticed that when we took her to Cambridge Roger was all dressed up in his most elaborate manners, a sure sign with him."

"He's very attractive," said Judith, smiling.

"Betty seems blind to his charms," admitted Roger's mother. "Of course she's seen him before, here and on visits and when he went down to school to see Marge. There's no newness about him for her. But she's grown up considerably since last he set eyes on her, so he thinks she's pretty keen. At least, so he said. But," she added, her eyes following Marge and Betty as they danced past the table with two young men who made up the party, "Marge tells me that Betty has a hopeless love. All in capitals, my dear! Who is it, do you know? I ask out of jealousy, for Roger's sake, not idle curiosity."

Judith said evenly:

"Her doctor — probably."

"Oh, of course, I don't blame her at all," said Mrs. Higgins. "I could go for that young man myself. We went to the hospital rather often when Betty was ill and I saw him . . . I forget his name . . . he was an intern there. Now I remember that when Marge came back from her Rivermount visit she told us that he was the hotel doctor now."

"Yes," said Judith.

"He's much too old for her, isn't he?" asked Mrs. Higgins, her blue eyes interested.

"He's thirty," said Judith, "and Betty doesn't think him a day too old."

"How about him?" asked Mrs. Higgins.

"I haven't the least idea," replied Judith a little shortly. Mrs. Higgins, by no means a stupid woman, looked at her, put two and two together and made eight. She made a small secret face at her husband which meant, Jimmy darling, it's time you danced with our guest.

He did so at once. It was no hardship.

On the following morning Judith was luxuriating in breakfast in bed. Very like old times. No duties, nothing. She sat back against the pillows, her hair tied up with a wide ribbon, a little jacket over her pretty gown. She regarded the tray, the delicate china and crystal, the rosebud in the little vase, with great satisfaction. A week in Boston, she decided, would make the life of a working girl ever so much harder, no matter how pleasant the conditions under which she worked.

Someone knocked, and came in. It was Clara Higgins, bearing a large square purple box.

"For me?" asked Judith, in utter amazement.

"For you. This minute. Mind if I stop and watch your reactions as you open it?"

Violets, a mass of them, fresh, dewy and scented with heaven. Judith buried her nose in them and sighed. Mrs. Higgins said critically, "To send violets to the guest of a very pro-Harvard family is little short of amusing but they go marvelously with your skin and hair. I wouldn't have believed it."

Judith laid them back in the box and fished for the card. Who on earth? No one knew she was here except — Bill. They couldn't be from Bill. She hoped desperately that they were. She hoped they were not. Crazy creature, what an extravagance!

They were not. In silence she read Bert Wallace's note.

"No Rivermount for me this weekend," it said. "I phoned when I read about the Benner matter. Thought perhaps a friendly word might cheer you, must have been nasty for you, my dear. Corbin told me where you'd gone so I came in on the last plane yesterday. How's for lunch with me today or dinner or whichever meal your hostess will spare you . . . or shall I come call formally?"

Judith made a little face. She gave the card to Clara Higgins and explained. "I've known him since I was an infant," she said, "his people had the next place to ours at Hillhigh. It's closed, as Mr. and Mrs. Wallace are away, but Bert spends weekends and his vacations at the hotel."

"Tell him to come for tea," said her hostess. "Where's he staying? Oh, I see, the Ritz. I'll telephone him if you like. And if you want to dine with him . . . we hadn't anything planned for you, specially. The youngsters were going off to dine and dance, at the Fanny Henshaw party. So Jim and I thought we'd take you out."

"You do far too much for me," said Judith gratefully.

"Not at all, we love it. Suppose we free you for your young man then?" suggested Clara.

Bert came to tea, comported himself with merit and the arrangements were made. He came back for her later and as the evening promised to be clear and fine they drove out to South Sudbury for dinner . . . a pleasant drive in a luxurious and chauffeured car.

"You do things," said Judith, at the old inn over an excellent dinner, "in a grand manner."

"Terribly upset, weren't you, by that Benner business?"

"Yes, rather," she told him.

"I wish you'd been spared it." He frowned and looked away. He'd sworn that this couldn't happen to him, but it was happening and there was nothing that he could do to prevent it. You set out to break a stubborn girl to your own will — why not, one more or less didn't matter, the world was full of girls — and she wouldn't break, she wouldn't even bend. So you went away and forgot her, with the same reasoning, why not, the world was full of girls. But you found that they didn't interest you much.

Not Candace, even, with her little flat in town and her golddigger proclivities. Bert rather admired her because of the way she handled things. Very cleverly. And she was attractive, more than attractive. She was quite beautiful with a strong and heady appeal to the senses, like a heavy perfume.

He'd had a rather amusing time with her. It had entertained him to permit her to become fairly sure of him. It would entertain him even more when she found that she wasn't sure at all. He looked forward to that.

But Judith. He'd thought about her, far too much for his own peace of mind. To his amazement he found that desire did not always die from lack of fuel. He had had everything he'd ever set his heart on. Except Judith. And there was only one way . . .

"Judy," he said, when they sat over coffee and cigarettes, "Judy, will you marry me?"

CHAPTER XIV

She looked at him a moment, too astonished to speak. He had paid her the highest compliment within his gift, the highest perhaps in any man's gift . . . unless the offer originated in the bottom of a highball glass. And for Bert — the perennial bachelor!

She said gently, "I'm sure you don't mean that, Bert."

"I do. I don't know what you were up to when you said that you were out after marriage. Whether it was true or not, won't I meet your requirements? I'm young enough," he said, and smiled at her, "and they tell me I'm not repulsive to look at. I have all it takes to support a wife. My parents like you very much, they will create no obstacle. In fact, the old man will be delighted. He wrote me not long ago that on the day I marry a girl of whom he approves he will hand over half a million in gilt-edged bonds . . . but that's neither here nor there. I —"

"You make it very tempting, don't you?" she asked. "Or you think you do. Am I really worth half a million in gilt-edged bonds and the sacrifice of your freedom, Bert?"

"I don't suppose any woman is," he replied calmly, "not really. But from where I sit you seem to be. So will you?"

She shook her head, smiling.

"I don't love you," she said.

"I love you," he told her, leaning closer, "enough for two. You — you would, after a while."

"That happens only in books."

"No, it doesn't. I know I got off on the wrong foot with you, Judy. But if you could forget it —"

"I've already forgotten it," she told him, "long ago." She looked at him, her eyes dancing. She was not very sorry for him. She believed in his powers of recuperation. "And you have certainly made the *amende honorable*. But, no thank you, I can't."

"It's Bill Martin," he said, scowling at her.

She was silent.

"You can't deny it, can you?"

"No," she confessed after a moment, raising her eyes to his, "I can't deny it and I don't want to. I am perfectly willing to admit it."

"Then he — and you —"

"Don't jump at conclusions," she advised him. "He's not in love with me. If he were, well, I wouldn't marry him either. You yourself know the reason, you advanced it once, didn't you? I couldn't do him any good. And he needs a wife who can help him. But, whether or not I am in love with him isn't the point, Bert. The point is, I'm *not* in love with you."

"And never will be?" he persisted.

"And never will be," she agreed.

"I wouldn't be too sure. I may get you on the rebound," he said.

She shook her head.

"I won't give up!" he warned her.

"Oh, yes," she said evenly, "you will. Not, of course, for a while. But your pride's too badly wounded to admit that." She regarded him with level eyes. The color rose in her cheeks but her eyes were steady. "You don't love me," she said softly. "I doubt if you will ever love anyone — much — except yourself. You — want me. That's different. And you know by now that you can't have me in any way but marriage. So you think you are willing to pay my particular price. You wouldn't be — long. And it isn't my price. So far as you are concerned I have none."

"You're crazy," he muttered, "and I'm crazy — about you."

"That," she said serenely, "just about covers it. Please" — she smiled at him again — "don't sit there and glower. You will be so grateful to me someday. You'll always remember me, probably, as the girl who saved you from —"

"Oh, stow it," he broke in sulkily, "you haven't any consideration for my feelings, Judy."

"Yes, I have," she contradicted. "And — — don't think I don't appreciate what you think you've offered me."

"What do you mean, what I *think?*"

"You'll have to figure that one out for yourself," she told him. "Hadn't we better start back now Bert?"

All the way back to Boston he argued with her. He made plans, he did everything but draw maps. They could be married at once, quietly, out in Chicago at Aunt Emily's if she insisted. They could go south . . . Virginia first, then Florida . . . or if she preferred, California. Then back, to sail for England and be with his people there for a while before returning in the spring and house hunting. An apartment in town, a place in the country.

Once she said:

"It's all very alluring but — it just doesn't add up to yes, Bert."

"You," he commented, "are the damnedest girl. I don't know why I put up with you."

"You said," she reminded him, "that you were in love with me."

"I don't know why I am either," he retorted. "We don't get on at all. You irritate me. Sometimes I dislike you very much. I'd like to shake you."

"You should," she said, and added hastily, "I didn't mean literally, Bert."

As he left her at the Higgins' door he said, "Well, as I told you before, I'm not quitting. See you tomorrow."

"I don't know what the Higgins' have planned," she began.

"That doesn't matter."

"And we're going back Monday," she reminded him.

"I'll call you," he said.

She noticed that the manservant who admitted her seemed shaken out of his usual calm. When the door closed behind Bert he said, with agitation:

"Mrs. Higgins was called away, Miss Gillmore."

Judith had her hands to her head, taking off her hat. She dropped the hat on a table and stood there still in her coat and asked quickly:

"What has happened, Leeds?"

"It's Mrs. Higgins's mother, an accident. Mr. and Mrs. Higgins left at once for New York. They are driving. There's a note here for you."

She read the note, confirming the butler's report. She said, after a moment, "Mrs. Higgins doesn't say if she wishes me to take Miss Marjorie on to New York or see that she gets a train."

"No, miss. Mrs. Higgins couldn't get in touch with Miss Marjorie, there wasn't time," explained Leeds, "and she told me that you were to tell her when she came in — it would be very late, she thought. She doesn't want her to follow her unless, when she telephones tomorrow, she thinks it's necessary."

"I see. All right," she told him, turning toward the stairs, "I'll wait up for her, Leeds, you may go to bed."

"Thank you, miss," he said gratefully and went away to his quarters, an elderly man, bent and a little tired, who had been in the family so long that he considered himself — and was — a part of it.

It was not yet very late. Judith, in her own pleasant room, took off her frock and brushed her hair. She put on a robe, and settled down to wait for the girls, with a new novel, and the radio turned low. There was milk in a thermos by her bed, and a plate of fruit and cookies. She thought, if I go to bed, I'll fall asleep.

She was, however, wide awake, reviewing mentally the events of the evening. Poor Bert! No, she wasn't very sorry for him. He'd rather steal than pay. But if he couldn't steal then he'd pay, reluctantly.

She would wait to hear from Mrs. Higgins tomorrow. If she wanted her to bring Marge on to New York she would. But girls nowadays went everywhere alone. Probably she would just put her on a train and then she and Betty would return to Rivermount.

Eventually she dozed over her book and, waking, found that it was nearly two o'clock. She was startled, waking in the strange room, finding herself fully dressed, save for her frock, the radio still on and the lights burning.

They will be coming home soon, she thought, glancing at the clock, and stretching her cramped legs and arms.

She rose from the chaise lounge and went over to the windows. While she was standing there, looking out, she heard the bell, ran out and downstairs to open the door. Marge was there, with one of the boys who had been with them the night before, but not Betty nor her escort.

Judith let them in. "Where's Betty?" she demanded.

"Betty?" Marge looked at her, open-mouthed. "But she came home ages ago."

"Ages — what do you mean?" demanded Judith. "She isn't here."

"But, Spud —" Marge turned to the astonished young man — "isn't that what she told us, when she called us off the floor? She had a bad headache and if I didn't mind she'd go on home, she said. Pat Dragsted said he'd take her . . . he was ducking out anyway to go to the Hamlin party."

"That's right," said Spud solemnly.

Judith thought fast. Aloud she said, "Well, probably it's nothing to worry about. Maybe she went on to the Hamlin party with Pat; things like that have happened before."

"I shouldn't wonder," said Marge, yawning. "Pat was trying to get us all to go. Fanny and Honor Hamlin hate each other. Last I saw of Betty she was saying good night to Fanny. I should have gone with her," she said self-consciously, "but she wouldn't hear of it."

"It's late," Judith reminded her. "She'll be along soon."

Spud knew a hint when he heard one. "Well, toodle-oo," he remarked, and cocked his hat on the side of his blond head.

" 'Night," said Marge sleepily, "I had a wonderful time."

But when he had gone and they were upstairs Judith would not let Marge go to her room. She took her in hers instead, and said, "Listen, Marge, I don't believe Betty went on to that party. We've got to find her. But first I have something to tell you."

"Betty didn't — what on earth — Oh, *Judith!*" cried Marge, her pretty little face stricken, "what's happened?"

"Your grandmother is very ill," Judith answered, sitting down beside her, "and your mother and father have gone to New York."

She gave her Mrs. Higgins's note and Marge looked up after reading it, her eyes full of tears. "Oh, poor Granny," she said, "she's such a darling. Is it — very bad?"

"I don't know any more than you do. Just what the note says, that she had a hard fall and broke her hip. Now, we can't telephone at this hour and worry them about Betty. And I don't want to upset her father if it's what I think it is. If it is I could spank her. I could anyway. You won't hear whether you're to go to New York or not, Marge, until tomorrow — later today I mean. And, so you can help me now — we have to find Betty."

"Where shall we start?" asked Marge, bug-eyed. "I thought she'd been acting very funny," she said. "She was nervous as a witch all evening . . . has been ever since she went out shopping alone the other day. Remember? When you and Mother went for a drive and I had to go to Dolly Talbot's?"

"Yes, I do remember now. Do you think the Hamlin party is still going on?"

"I wouldn't know. I had an invitation. Wait, I'll find it." She ran off to her room and returned with the card in her hand. "I could call the hotel."

"Do," said Judith. "Ask if they can page Pat What's-his-name and get him to the phone."

Marge sat down at the telephone in Judith's room. After a short wait she was connected with the hotel. The party was still going on. But after a much longer wait she was informed that Mr. Dragsted could not be found.

"Call his house," said Judith swiftly. "If you get him, tell him you are very sorry to disturb him at this hour but — wait a minute — yes, that's it — ask if Betty dropped her bracelet in his car. She wore one, didn't she?"

"Her graduation present, diamonds and sapphires," said Marge. "I fastened it for her."

"Ask him if he saw it. Tell him not to bother to look in the car tonight. We'll phone again tomorrow. Just ask if he recalls her having it on . . . and then ask him to more or less retrace their steps."

"I understand," said Marge swiftly.

She called the Dragsted house and after a few moments reached Pat. Judith, almost ill with nervousness, listened to Marge's side of the conversation which didn't convey much.

"Well?" she asked, as Marge hung up.

The youngster was quite white and her eyes were big and startled. "He said he saw the bracelet —"

"Never mind about the bracelet, what about Betty?"

"That was it. He said that she wouldn't let him drive her right up to the house, as he would have to turn again — to go on to the hotel. She made him let her off at the corner, across the street. She had to wait for the traffic signal. He said he noticed the bracelet on her arm as she got out and waved to him. He just got home a moment ago."

"That settles it," said Judith with determination. "He did bring her home, or almost home. But she had no intention of coming back. She has eloped with Saks Lewis."

"Saks Lewis!" gasped Marge. "But she won't even give him a —"

"I know," said Judith. She was dressing with incredible swiftness. "Get the Ritz on the telephone, ask to be connected with Mr. Albert Wallace."

She couldn't call Rivermount, it would be hours before Mr. Corbin could reach them. By that time Saks and Betty would be married . . . or would they? Where could they be married, in what state, at this time of night? Where at any time without notice? Rhode Island, perhaps? Maryland? But so many states had tightened their marriage laws and abolished their Gretna Greens.

Her heart was heavy with fear but she found that her nervousness had left her. If Bill were only here — yet Bill was the last person to whom she could turn in the circumstances. Bert should be of assistance if only because he had the means at his command.

Marge was talking, "Mr. Wallace, I'm calling for Miss Gillmore . . ."

Judith took the instrument from her. She said swiftly, "I'm sorry, Bert, but I need your help. Can you get over here — yes, to the Higgins house, as soon as possible?"

When she had hung up she called the hotel at which Saks played for dancing. The grill was closed at this hour but she talked to an intelligent night clerk. Yes, they had midnight closing on Saturdays. No dancing after midnight. No, Mr. Lewis did not live in the hotel but he could get her the address. She waited until he had read it to her, wrote it on the telephone pad, thanked him and hung up.

"Saks must have left there something just after midnight," she told Marge, "and then come here to wait for Betty. They have over two hours' start."

"What are you going to do?" asked Marge, half crying, watching Judith make herself ready for the street.

"Find them as soon as possible."

"Would Mr. Corbin be wild if she married Saks?" asked Marge.

"He probably wouldn't like it. There isn't anything against Saks, of course, he's a nice boy really," said Judith. "But Betty doesn't want to marry him."

"You mean that she's in love with Dr. Martin," said Marge, nodding. "Of course!"

"Oh," said Judith, exasperated, "I can't understand her!"

"But she knows that Dr. Martin's in love with you, Judy," said Marge, a little hesitantly.

"She knows nothing of the kind!" cried Judith, whirling on her. "I can't help what she thinks . . . it's all so idiotic. I can't have her running off marrying a boy she doesn't love because of what she thinks. And it isn't fair to either of them."

"But she told me," persisted Marge. "I'm her very best friend and she told me — she saw you in Dr. Martin's arms, he was kissing you and saying —"

Judith stood stock-still and stared at her. "There isn't a word of truth in that, Marge," she said, too stunned to say more.

"But why would she . . . ? Oh, there's the bell."

"Run down," said Judith, "and let him in. I'll be right there."

Following Marge, she thought, If Betty said that? But she couldn't. She had no reason. Or *had* she seen someone? Whom had she seen . . . in Bill's arms? There wasn't anyone. Or — was there?

Bert was in the hall, looking bewildered but ready for any emergency. And Judith explained as briefly as possible. "Marge," she concluded, turning to the younger girl, "you'd better go to bed. I'll phone you the first opportunity I have. If your mother calls before — there is no use upsetting her — simply say that we've returned to Rivermount. I will explain it to her later. But I hope I'll be back with Betty long before then." She stopped and kissed the girl's round cheek.

"Stiff upper lip," she recommended, "you've been — swell. If you're afraid to be alone, wake Mrs. Leeds and have her sleep in Betty's room. I'll call you as soon as possible."

She put her hand on the girl's shoulder and then turned to Bert. "Let's go," she said.

"Taxi waiting," he told her. "Where to, first?"

"To Saks Lewis's hotel," she answered.

CHAPTER XV

In the taxi she explained hurriedly.

"I thought the people where he lives might know something . . . probably the boys in his orchestra live there too."

"Relax," advised Bert, "why all this excitement? Betty's eighteen, isn't she? She can marry whom she pleases."

"That's just it," said Judith distractedly, "she doesn't please! She's just doing this out of —"

"Well, go on."

"Childish nonsense," amended Judith firmly. "And I feel terribly responsible."

"Why? Do your duties at the hotel include a goddess-from-the-machine attitude toward the manager's daughter? And what a machine! Hurry, can't you?" he demanded, rapping on the glass between them and the driver.

"I'm chaperoning Betty during her visit here," explained Judith evasively.

"I thought her friend's parents were —"

"Stop quibbling," she ordered, exasperated, "and they're in New York anyway."

The taxi jerked to a stop at the small

hotel in which Lewis lived during this Boston engagement. It was on a side street in the theater district. Bert got out and paid the driver. He told Judith, as they walked into the lobby, "If we are going on a boy-and-girl hunt we'll get a car from one of the all-night garages."

Judith, hurrying ahead of him through the dimly lighted, rather dingy lobby, went straight to the desk to make her inquiries. The weasel-eyed clerk was inclined to be insolent until Wallace's large frame loomed up behind her, after which he was more courteous. Yes, Mr. Lewis lived there. No, he didn't know whether or not he was in. And he didn't believe that he could ring his room at this hour. As a matter of fact, now that he thought of it, he was sure Mr. Lewis hadn't come in.

"We can wait," said Bert.

That did not suit the Weasel at all. He explained hastily that sometimes Mr. Lewis did not come in until morning. Often he and his men went from their hotel engagement to a private party or a special shindig at some club and played the rest of the night.

Bert leaned across the counter. He displayed a bill carelessly. He said, "We aren't dicks if that's what's worrying you. We are friends of Mr. Lewis and" — he took a long chance — "the young lady."

The clerk eyed them warily. No, they were too young to be outraged parents. The bill skittered across the worn counter. He said reluctantly, "Well, I'll ring his room."

"No," said Bert, "just tell me his number. The house phone's right there, isn't it?" Before the clerk could do more than say "three hundred and four," he had usurped the instrument and was talking to the night operator.

"Hello," he said presently, while Judith waited, very pale, her hands twisted together. "Hello — that you, Lewis?"

He nodded at Judith and her heart gave a great upward leap. He went on talking. "Bert Wallace . . . yes. No, never mind all that. We're coming up."

He hung up and said briefly, "Let's go."

They walked toward the elevator, the clerk looking after them in some perturbation. He hoped to heaven there wouldn't be a row. There hadn't been one since the snake charmer had brought her snakes along and one had escaped, to the horror of the gentleman in the next room, on the verge of d.t.'s.

On the way up Bert told Judith, low.

"He was — astonished. I woke him up, he said. Couldn't imagine what I wanted. Did his best to keep us from coming up. Said he'd dress and come down."

"Bert, what do you suppose — ?"

"We'll soon know."

He knocked vigorously at the door marked 304. It was opened instantly and Saks Lewis stood there. He was fully dressed and looked haggard and unhappy. Bert stepped in, pulled Judith in with him and closed the door.

Judith spoke first.

"Where's Betty?" she asked.

"Betty? I haven't the least idea," replied Saks defensively. "How should I know?"

She certainly wasn't in the room, which was fairly good-sized, cheaply furnished but comfortable enough. The single bed had not been slept in. A traveling bag was half open on the luggage rack, ties and socks spilling out of it. A bright ceiling light burned, the room was full of smoke, and an ash tray held a dozen crushed out cigarette ends.

"Listen," said Bert, "it's no good stalling. You'd better come clean, Lewis." Judith listened, amazed and half inclined to laugh despite her fear and anxiety. For Bert was talking like someone in the movies, and

224

out of the corner of his mouth. He was vastly enjoying his role, she realized. "We know that Betty's with you. Didn't you think Judith would find out, when she didn't come home and Judith questioned the youngster who was supposed to bring her? It was dollars to doughnuts that she'd met you. Well, speak up, what's happened to her? Do you realize what this is going to mean to you? Alex Corbin has plenty of influence. He'll get you blacklisted in every hotel in the country. A scandal at the beginning of your so-called career won't help you any, Lewis."

The boy's tired young face broke into lines of misery. He looked piteously at Judith. His eyes, she saw, were rimmed with red.

"Wait a minute," she said, "let me talk to him." She went over and put her hand on his arm. She asked gently:

"Saks, won't you help us — and Betty? You love her, don't you?"

He nodded, swallowing convulsively.

"Then — you'll prove it? You'll tell us where she is, what happened. You were going to elope, weren't you?"

"Yes," he said, finding his voice and it sounded thin and harsh, "yes, we were." He ignored Bert, and spoke directly to Judith. "I — I asked her to marry me a dozen times this summer. But she wouldn't; she didn't love me, she was in love with —"

Judith broke in swiftly.

"When was this elopement arranged?"

"I met her the other afternoon. She called me, here. She knew where I lived. I went to Jordan Marsh's and met her. We went to a little restaurant and had some tea. She said she was terribly unhappy. She said she would marry me, if I'd run away with her. I argued that there wasn't any reason why we couldn't be engaged — and married, regularly, you know. I thought I could win her father over. He likes me all right, even if he was sore because Betty started going around with me in the summer. But she wouldn't have it that way. It was this way, at once, or not at all. So we planned. She was always with you or Marge or someone but then I hit on to-night. I knew she was going to the dance and suggested she manage to slip away after midnight, when I'd be through at the hotel and could wait for her. It all happened just as we planned. She couldn't bring much with her without attracting attention, but during the afternoon she packed a little bag and checked it in the Back Bay Station. I don't know how she got out with it —"

"She went to the hairdresser's," said Judith, remembering, "and took a taxi. I was out with Mrs. Higgins and Marge, shopping. We all met at tea."

"I had a taxi waiting," said Saks. "We went to the station, got the bag and came back here so that I could get mine. I changed my clothes after I was through playing tonight but I forgot to take the bag along."

"Well?" Judith asked impatiently, "Saks, for heaven's sake, where *is* she?"

"She's here," he answered, "down the hall, in three hundred and ten. I was such a fool. I didn't find out if we could be married in this state tonight, without notice. We couldn't. And anyway, there wasn't a license bureau open. I hadn't thought about that," he went on. "I talked to Jake, the night clerk. And the upshot was I got her a room here for tonight. We were going to take the car and drive, perhaps to Maryland, tomorrow . . . that is, today."

"Were going?" asked Judith shrewdly.

"We quarreled," he said miserably, "and — Oh, hell, such a mess," he added looking from the obviously amused older man to Judith, "she says now that she won't marry me, that she never wants to see me again — but that she can't go back home."

Judith ordered, "You two stay here!"

She was out the door and up the hall to 310 before either man had moved. She knocked. There was no answer. She knocked again and listened. She thought she heard a deep, broken sound such as a child makes when it is worn out from crying. Then:

"Go away!" said Betty, from the room.

"It's Judy," said Judith softly.

There was a moment of silence. Then Betty said, with an attempt at belligerence:

"Go 'way just the same. This isn't your business."

Judith said swiftly, firmly:

"Betty, I can't stand here the rest of the night. I'll disturb other people. You must let me in. If you don't I shall be forced to ring for the manager and ask him to use his pass key."

"Oh, all right," said Betty, defeated.

There was a moment's wait, the sound of a key being turned and the door opened. Judith went in and closed it behind her. "Lock it," said Betty fiercely, "I don't want *him* coming in here."

Judith obeyed. Then she walked over to the bed where Betty was now sitting, and looked down on her.

The child was very white. Her fair hair was in disorder, powder had caked on her cheeks, her lip rouge was smeared. She still wore her pretty dance frock. She had kicked off her stilt-heeled silver slippers; they lay on the floor. Her bag was on the chair, unopened; her evening wrap was thrown over the back. On the rumpled bed were half a dozen crumpled handkerchiefs.

Judith sat down and put her arm around her.

"You're going home," she said.

"Home? But I can't. Mrs. Higgins —" Betty paused and choked — "she wouldn't ever let me see Marge again!" she said mournfully.

"Why?"

"I've been out all night," cried Betty, looking at her with round, frightened eyes. "I eloped — and didn't get married. I'm not going to get married. I'll — I'll go away and find a job somewhere, on my own," she concluded.

Judith suppressed a smile.

"No one," she told Betty, "except Marge and I, Bert Wallace and Saks know that you've been out all night . . . except possibly Mrs. Leeds, and she won't tell —"

"What do you mean?" gasped Betty. "Haven't the Higginses —"

"They're in New York," said Judith. She explained briefly. She concluded, "And now you're coming back to Marge's house with us."

"But Saks —" began Betty.

"I wouldn't blame Saks too much, Betty. After all, it was your idea and he's in love with you. He's wretched, poor fellow."

"He shouldn't have taken me up," said Betty illogically, "he should have known I didn't mean it. I was — Oh, well, it was just craziness. I wanted to get away, from everybody, everything. Then we came here, and it was all so sort of cheap and creepy and — dirty somehow. I hated it. And we couldn't be married tonight. If we could have been, right away . . . but we couldn't and he got me this room. So I said I didn't want to see him again, ever, and I've been sitting here ever since."

"We're getting out now," said Judith firmly, "and we'll discuss it all tomorrow. Meantime, put your things on. That's right, don't forget your slippers! Give me your bag."

"I don't have to see Saks?" begged Betty, shrinking against her.

"Not if you don't want to. Not now, at all events." She marshaled Betty from the room. "Go to the elevator at the end of the hall and wait," she told her. "And remember, I trust you not to run out on me."

"I haven't any money," admitted Betty, "just change for the hat-check girl at the dance. I couldn't run out on anyone."

Judith watched her walking away from her toward the elevator. She knocked on Saks' door and it was flung open. She said swiftly, as both men stepped toward her:

"Bert, go catch up with Betty by the elevator, will you? Take her downstairs and to a taxi. I'll follow at once. I want to speak to Saks."

Bert nodded and went on out, and Judith, closing the door, faced the orchestra leader.

"So far," she said, "so good. And no harm done." But it was almost a question.

"No harm done," he said quietly. "But her father," he added, looking, "will he believe that?"

"I don't think there's any reason for him to know," said Judith making up her mind in the second which elapsed between question and answer. "I'll talk to Betty tomorrow. There's no sense, now, in talking. She's too tired and overwrought. You've been exceptionally stupid," she added severely.

"Don't I know it? I should have had more sense. But — Lord, Judith, it was my chance. At least I thought so. If only she'd marry me, I kept telling myself, I'd make her happy, she'd love me."

Judith shook her head.

"Things don't always work out that way," she reminded him.

"Now," he said wretchedly, "I'll never see her again."

"Perhaps not. But perhaps you will," said Judith. "Women are curious, you know. The day may come when she'll look back on this episode as the most romantic thing that ever happened to her. When she does, if she does, your star will be in the ascendant. But I can't promise you that, Saks. It's up to Betty."

He said, "Judith, you've been such a brick. I don't know how I can thank you."

"You should hate me," she said, smiling.

"No, I don't. I realized before you came that morning wouldn't bring a solution, it would just make things worse. She still wouldn't want to marry me and if she did it would be because she would be afraid to go home and had nowhere else to go. And I didn't want her that way."

"No," she said, "of course you didn't."

At the door she turned. "I'll settle for the room," she said, "downstairs."

"It's paid for," he told her, with a twisted

smile. "Everything's paid for."

She asked, at the door:

"Call the Higgins house, will you? Marge will answer. Tell her Betty and I are on our way home. You needn't say any more. But I don't want her to worry a single minute more than I can help."

"All right," he said docilely.

She looked at him and smiled. She felt so very much older and wiser and so eternally grateful that chance had helped her solve this particular problem. He looked so young, younger than Betty, this lonely, romantic lad who could make a saxophone talk, who could coax crazy, exciting, glowing music out of a group of men and instruments. She wondered what lay before him, and how much of a blow to his pride this night had been. But not alone to his pride, she thought, walking away, remembering her last sight of him, disheveled, disconsolate. For that he was really in love with the girl who, having run away with him, was now running away from him, Judith did not doubt.

CHAPTER XVI

Betty and Bert were waiting in the taxi. On the way to the Higgins', Bert made light conversation, offered cigarettes. Betty refused but Judith took one. She needed it. She felt very tired.

When the cab drew up, "See you tomorrow — today?" asked Bert, holding her hand closely in his own.

She shook her head. "No, I think not," she told him. "For if Marge has to go to New York, Betty and I will return to Hillhigh. In fact, we may anyway. Thanks a lot, Bert, for all you've done. I needn't ask you to —"

"I'll keep my mouth shut," he said lightly. "Okay, then, Judy. See you next weekend."

Marge, in a bathrobe, opened the door. She had been watching at the window ever since Saks' telephone call reached her.

Now they were safe, inside the big friendly house. Betty gave one wild look around her and burst into tears.

"Take her upstairs," said Judith. She thought, Betty doesn't like me any better for this, but Marge is her closest friend and her own age. "And get her to bed . . . and don't let her talk."

Marge nodded, too relieved for curiosity. And Judith watched the two girls, their arms around each other, trail up the stairs. She turned out the lights and followed, going directly to her own room, almost dropping from weariness. She had undressed when Marge came in.

"She's in bed," she reported, "she's still crying. Judy, what happened?"

"Very little. They met as they'd planned, and we guessed, and went to the place where Saks lives to pick up his bag and by then they had realized that they couldn't get married at this time of night, especially without a license. Also, by then, Betty discovered that she didn't want to marry him, so the trip to Maryland in the morning was definitely out. But she was afraid to come here — or go home."

"Gosh," said Marge, on a deep breath. "I'm so glad it turned out this way. You're simply swell, Judy," she told the older girl.

"I didn't do anything," said Judith. "It was all done for me."

"Look — are you going to tell Mr. Corbin?"

"I think not," answered Judith slowly.

235

She was very much disturbed over the necessity for this decision. She was under great obligation to Alex Corbin. She felt, in a measure, responsible for all that had happened. Yet she wasn't much older than Betty — and Saks was even her senior. She had to be on the side of youth. Besides, what was there to be gained? She said finally, "I'll talk to Betty when she's in some condition to discuss things sensibly."

"Boy, you are *swell!*" said Marge again, her limited vocabulary inadequate to the occasion.

Judith went to her dressing table and picked up a little bottle. She said, shaking a white tablet into her palm, "I'll give her this, it's just a mild sedative."

Standing there with the bottle in her hand she thought of Bill who had given her the medicine. Thought of him, and felt her heart wrench in her breast. Someday she would have to ask Betty, straight out from the shoulder, what had she meant by telling Marge that absurd lie.

She went to Betty's room and found her in bed, her nose and eyes swollen and her breathing unsteady. She offered her the tablet and a glass of water. "Don't try to talk tonight," she said, "just — sleep if you can." She tucked her in and went across the room to open the windows. "There," she said, "you're all set."

Betty said in a small, unwilling voice, "I haven't thanked you."

"You don't have to."

"Will Mr. Wallace . . ." Betty began.

"He won't say anything. Why should he?"

"Marge won't either. But the servants?"

"Marge told me that she did not call Mrs. Leeds as I suggested, so the story will be that you went on to the other party and remained very late. You have nothing to worry about, Betty."

But Judith worried, for the brief remainder of the night.

In the morning, early, Clara Higgins telephoned her. Would she put Marge on a train? Marge's grandmother was in a serious condition, she had asked to see her. But of course Betty and Judith must stay on as long as they wished to, the servants would look after them.

No, Judith said, they were to return to Hillhigh tomorrow in any event. They would simply get a train today instead. One left around the time the New York train pulled out, she thought. And Mrs. Higgins wasn't to worry. Marge would be on the train, everything would be all right.

They were too busy before traintime to talk very much, packing, looking at time-tables, wiring Mr. Corbin. Betty and Marge were heavy-eyed but, with the resilience of youth, a few hours' sleep had seemed to suffice them. And Judith as well. She felt rested and extraordinarily relieved. She had made up her mind.

The Higgins car had gone to New York, so a taxi took them all to the station. Betty and Judith saw Marge off on her train, the two girls embraced each other, they would write soon, they promised. And Marge kissed Judith shyly. "You're grand," she said, smiling a little mistily.

On the long trip to Hillhigh there was plenty of time for conversation. There were few people in the parlor car on Sunday, they were traveling the wrong way for crowds. Betty complained of a headache and Judith arranged for them to occupy the empty drawing room rather than their chairs. They were quiet there, and se-cluded. There was a diner aboard and at lunchtime Judith ordered tea and club sandwiches and watched Betty revive slightly. She did not open the discussion, she waited for the younger girl to do that. And after the porter had cleared away, Betty, against her white pillow, looking out the window said, without turning:

"I suppose you'll tell Father."

"No," said Judith.

"You won't!"

"I see no reason to. No one is going to tell anything, Betty, unless you'd rather. Marge won't, Bert Wallace won't, the servants know nothing, Marge's parents are in New York, and Saks —"

"Don't mention his name!" cried Betty.

"You mustn't be childish," said Judith. "Why not? He was in love with you, Betty, he still is. And, after all, the elopement suggestion came from you."

"It was all so different from what I expected," said the romanticist sadly. She thought, Perhaps I'll lose weight and pine away. I'll be ill and Bill will have to take care of me. He'll be sorry for me, perhaps he'll even —

But Judith was speaking.

She said, "Had you succeeded in leaving Boston headed for heaven knows where, of course your father would have to be told. But as you didn't — Sometime you may want to tell him of your own accord but I see no reason to disturb and trouble him now."

"I thought you'd tell," said Betty.

"Why?"

"Oh, I don't know. But I knew if you told I couldn't bear it. I — I'd run away, I'd kill myself!" she said dramatically.

"No, you wouldn't," said Judith flatly, "don't be absurd."

"I don't think it's absurd," said Betty sulkily.

She should be grateful to Judith. She was — of course. But she couldn't rave about her the way Marge did. Marge was too sickening the way she raved. And she couldn't forget about Bill — and what she'd seen. Just because Judith had got her out of a jam Betty couldn't turn around and fall on her neck and weep, I'm so glad Bill's in love with you!

She was a perfectly normal young thing with normal reactions.

"Of course not," said Judith soothingly. "Honestly, Betty, the best thing to do is to forget all about this. There'll be plenty of excitement going on at Rivermount. You'll have a grand time this winter. And you're going to Boston again to stay with Marge when she makes her debut."

"If her grandmother dies that will have to be postponed, I suppose," mourned Betty with the supreme and comprehensible selfishness of her years.

"Perhaps. But the other day Mrs. Higgins said something about taking Marge abroad in the spring and hoping that your father would let you go with them."

Color sprang to Betty's cheeks, her eyes were brilliant. She looked eager and greedy and very pretty. She cried, all animation, "Oh, Judy, truly? How perfectly wonderful. Do you think he'll let me?"

"I shouldn't wonder," Judith answered, smiling.

"How too marvelous," said Betty, wrapped in dreams, "if only I could. I've always wanted to go abroad." Then she was silent. Her animation faded. She thought, but if I go — and leave Bill? She said in a small voice, primly, "I don't deserve it."

"Probably we don't any of us deserve the good things that come our way," agreed Judith, laughing.

"Perhaps I shouldn't even consider it," said Betty, "as a — a sort of punishment for being so silly."

"You wait till the time comes," advised Judith, "and then see how you feel. Spring's a long way off."

There was a long silence. Betty thought, Well, anyway, I haven't a chance with Bill. Maybe I should go away and forget!

She saw herself trailing around Europe smiling sadly at handsome earls, dukes, counts and barons . . . a blonde with a Past (Saks) and with a Hidden Grief (Bill). The picture had its charm.

Later Judith plucked up her courage to ask Betty the question which had been troubling her.

"Betty —"

"Well?"

"Will you tell me something honestly?"

"But I've told you everything," said Betty, astonished.

"I didn't mean that. Will you tell me why you told Marge that you saw me and Bill Martin —" she stopped and colored clear to the roots of her lovely hair — "that you saw him kissing me?" she ended awkwardly.

"But you — I —" Betty stared at her open-mouthed, and Judith hurried on.

"It wasn't true, Betty. He never has. It was such a stupid, meaningless thing to say, my dear."

"I could wring Marge's neck," said Betty slowly. She thought, Then she *was* unconscious. She didn't know! She didn't hear!

She thought further, *Why should I tell her?*

Aloud she said:

"I'm sorry, Judy. It was just one of those things."

"But there wasn't any point to it," said Judy soberly. "If you saw him with someone, it wasn't with me."

"I didn't see him at all," Betty said calmly, and Judith's heart lifted on a wave of relief. "I just made it up."

"Why?"

"Oh," she answered carelessly, "Marge is so romantic. She thought that you — you and Bill, you know. So — I made it up."

That, thought Judith, isn't the reason. I'll never know the reason.

She shrugged her slim shoulders and lighted a cigarette.

"All right," she said, "but it was pretty ridiculous, Betty. And if it ever got back to him —"

"It won't," said Betty eagerly, "and I'm truly so sorry, Judy."

There. She had paid her back . . . for being efficient and clever and for her few superior years. If she was so senseless, so unemotional, so cold, thought Betty, that she wouldn't come right back to life when Bill Martin held her in his arms and kissed her, she didn't deserve to have him kiss her. To be perfectly truthful, Betty didn't know whether he had kissed her or not. She had simply seen Judith in his arms and had heard him speak to her. "Judith, my darling," he had said.

Betty was very glad to be home again. Bill was waiting for them in the cold dark night, brilliant with stars. Mr. Corbin, he explained, driving them back to the hotel, was busy with new arrivals, a whole houseful, a convention of females, and had sent him instead. How well they looked . . . but a little tired. Had they been very dissipated? And how, he wanted to know especially, was Judith?

"Completely recovered," reported Judith serenely, sitting there beside him — no, not beside him as Betty was between them on the front seat, and thinking how little it took to make her happy.

"Bert Wallace said he'd never seen you look better," Betty reminded her.

It was true, of course, Bert had made the comment on the afternoon he came for tea.

The car swerved a little. Bill asked evenly:

"Wallace was — in Boston?"

Judith thought, I could shake her. Not that Bill cares whether Bert was in Boston or not, but it's none of Betty's business. She answered casually, "Yes, he flew up. Came to the Higgins's for tea and I dined with him. He came to tell me how sorry he was about . . . By the way, did — did everything straighten out?" she wanted to know.

"Benner, you mean. Yes, his people came. I'm glad you weren't there," he told her somberly, "it was pretty — tragic."

"We had a grand time," Betty broke in, sitting there very close beside him, "but I'm awfully glad I'm home."

"See Saks?" he asked carelessly and it was Judith who answered, quickly:

"Yes, indeed. We went to the place where he plays."

"Nice kid," said Bill, chewing on an unlighted pipe. "Been dull here since you girls left," he told them. "All work and no play. But I didn't mind the work. Had a dozen cases of ptomaine in the village. Believe it or not, it was because of an oyster supper at the church. Quite a scandal, in these parts."

"Have you seen your aunt?" Judith demanded.

"Yes, ma'am, I have. I went to her back door and delivered your message. She listened in silence. Then she slammed the door in my face. I doubt if you'll get in again . . . you made a strategic error in sending me around and it's the last time I'll go," he concluded grimly.

"Oh," cried Judith, "poor Aunt Hetty!"

Betty listened, glowering. She felt left out of everything, she didn't fit here at all. What in the world did Judith know about Bill's aunt?

Monday was Judith's day off. But she had had a week, so she stayed at her desk and directed the amusements she had planned before leaving for the convention of clubwomen who had taken over the hotel. Riding, driving, a picnic in the mountain cabin which belonged to the hotel, motion pictures, a card game, all between club meetings. But a little after five o'clock when there was nothing further to do and, feeling in need of air and exercise, she went to her room to put on a pullover and a suéde jacket and go for a walk before dinner. She had a letter to her mother ready, she might as well take it to the post office.

Dusk came early now and even in October the heavy blue-black clouds over the mountains threatened snow. The air was very cold, there was a brisk wind and Judith walked fast, to keep warm. She mailed her letter and was turning back when an impulse took her past Aunt Hetty's cottage. She could at least look in on the old woman and if, as Bill thought, she was angry, she could apologize. But she didn't believe that Aunt Hetty was really angry.

A light burned, in the back. The front of the house was dark. Judith went to the kitchen door and knocked. There was no answer. She was turning away when the door swung a little, creaking on its hinges. It hadn't been locked, then, it had been ajar. She turned back, pushed it open and stepped across the threshold.

"Miss Martin," she called.

There was no answer. But she heard someone breathing heavily. She saw the tortoise-shell cat leap across the floor and come to rub himself against her legs. Filled with gathering uneasiness, she went through the kitchen and into the passage.

Aunt Hetty lay there, huddled against the wall, her limbs twisted, her gray hair in wild disorder. And there was blood on her lined forehead.

CHAPTER XVII

There was no telephone in Hetty Martin's house. Judith, making a superhuman effort, got the small slight woman into her strong young arms and carried her, a dead weight, through the passage and into a bedroom off the kitchen where she put her on the bed. The cat followed, crying, aware of disaster as cats always seem to be.

She ran out and down the street to Miss Martin's next-door neighbor and knocked on the back door. A thin, dour woman answered, wiping her hands on her apron, and Judith said breathlessly:

"Miss Martin has had an accident. She's unconscious. Have you a phone?"

"Yes," said the woman. She added grudgingly, "I ain't spoken to Hetty Martin for going on eleven years and I don't aim to begin now. But I'll do what I can."

"I'll call the doctor," said Judith, "if you'll show me where —"

The woman indicated the telephone, in the kitchen. She listened to Judith calling the hotel. "Hurry, central, please hurry!"

248

and said "I'll go over now and stay with her while you telephone."

When she had established her connection Judith asked frantically, "Is that you, Elsie? Has Dr. Martin come in yet?"

"Dr. Martin? Oh, it's Miss Gillmore. Yes, he's in his office," said the hotel operator. "I'll put him right on."

Bill had hardly managed to say hello before she cut in. "It's Judith . . . come as fast as you can," she cried, "Aunt Hetty has had an accident."

He didn't even answer. He simply hung up, and she went racing back to find Miss Martin still unconscious and the neighbor standing by the bed.

"Looks like a shock to me," she said calmly.

"I've sent for Dr. Martin — her nephew," explained Judith.

The neighbor, who presently introduced herself as Mrs. Thomas, shook her head.

"She'd have to be unconscious to let him in the house," she commented. "The way she's treated that boy's a caution! Nice boy too. And, I hear, a good doctor. I've always stuck to the old doctor myself," she added, sitting down beside the bed, "but he's almost eighty and maybe a change would help my rheumatism some."

Judith pressed her hands together.

"Oh, why doesn't he hurry!" she said miserably.

"If I was him," said Mrs. Thomas, "I wouldn't come at all."

Judith looked at her. "He's a doctor," she said; "it doesn't matter what his relationship to Miss Martin is — he has to come!"

Mrs. Thomas shrugged her spare shoulders.

"She put up a spite fence," she said, "because my dog chased her blasted cats. We was friends, years ago." She looked down at the woman on the bed. "Well," she said reluctantly, "poor thing, looks like she's got her comeuppance for all her meanness."

Miss Hetty stirred and moaned.

"I think she's coming to," whispered Judith.

But the alteration was momentary, for Miss Hetty lapsed into unconsciousness again.

When Judith, listening, heard Bill's car draw up, she ran to the front door and flung it open. He said, "Well, what's all this?" unprepared for her sudden clinging to him.

"I've been so frightened," she said, in excuse. "I thought perhaps she was dead, I found her in the hall."

Bill put his arm around her and together they went back into the bedroom. Mrs. Thomas, still sitting there, interested but motionless, said, "Well, Bill," unemotionally, and he answered mechanically, "How are you, Miss Sarah?" and she explained, in an aside to Judith, "He used to call me that. I married Thomas late. Too late, I sometimes think."

Judith wasn't listening.

"Oh, Bill what is it?" she demanded.

"You run along out," he told her. "Miss Sarah will stay here with me. She's used to sickness."

"Had my mother-in-law with the palsy, six years," said Mrs. Thomas.

Judith went out slowly. She was shaking, a little. She thought dismally, Well, I'm not much good around emergencies, am I?

Miss Hetty's parlor was prim. Turning on a light, Judith saw a horsehair sofa. It looked slippery and uncomfortable. There were enlarged crayons of melancholy-looking ladies and gentlemen on the walls. A round table, a lamp, a Bible, a wax wreath under glass. The cat came sneaking across the Brussels carpet and jumped into her lap. It was a stiff, sad little room. She looked up at one picture and noticed the resemblance to Bill despite the bad photography and old-fashioned clothes. She hadn't, then, discarded all traces of her brother.

Bill came in, his face set. "She's had a stroke," he said, "and I'm at my wits' end what to do. If I take her to the hospital . . . Miss Sarah says that she'll fight it, tooth and nail, when she comes to. Expense and all. I couldn't put her in a ward, I'd get a private room and nurses for her and pay for them — but if she'd be unhappy there — On the other hand, she can't be here alone."

"Hank's daughter Rose," said Judith eagerly, "is home on a vacation. She's not a graduate, of course, but she's had a couple of years' training. She might take over until you could get someone else who'd come in and stay. I would come in every day."

"That might be the best thing," he agreed, his face clearing. "I've got a practical nurse, an excellent, middle-aged woman, Mrs. Ellis, on a pneumonia case now; my patient is better, she could leave in a few days. She'd take over everything, on a twenty-four hour duty basis. Meantime if Rose could help us out? And I'll stay here tonight."

"I'll run down to Parsons'," offered Judith.

In less than half an hour she was back with Rose, a pretty, stocky girl with good hands and a quiet, competent way about her. Rose was perfectly willing to help until Mrs. Ellis came off her case. She was, she admitted, getting tired of doing nothing. And Judith, seeing the frank blue-eyed smile with which she favored Bill, decided that he'd have no trouble in getting nurses to work for him — ever.

Her mother would send up hot meals, Rose told Bill. "Don't you worry about me," she added.

Mrs. Thomas, promising to do anything she could, went back home — to call all her friends on the party line and tell them the latest news. And after a time Bill came out of the sickroom again, leaving Rose in charge. "I'll stop at the drugstore," he said, "and then drive you home, Judith. Later I'll come back and stay with Aunt Hetty overnight."

"Is it very bad?"

"I don't think so," he said, "I think it will clear. Her right side is paralyzed, however."

"Oh, Bill, how dreadful for her!"

"How fortunate that you happened by

when you did," he said soberly, "otherwise she might not have been found till morning. The house would have been cold, no one to tend the fire. Not ever having been neighborly, people wouldn't have been apt to run in, even seeing a light burn in the kitchen all night. Judith, how on earth did you get her into the bedroom?"

"I carried her."

"But . . ."

"I'm strong," she said, "and she's a little thing. Bill, the blood on her forehead?"

"Struck her head, falling," he said, "it doesn't amount to anything. I'm sure she'll be all right. As soon as she's out of the woods I'll call in someone else. I'll have Dr. Smith over from Valleytown tonight in consultation, and he can take over if she likes. She'll hate to have me around when she's conscious," he said bitterly.

"Bill, don't feel like that."

"How else am I to feel?" he demanded.

The days went on, growing shorter, the dark came early and toward the end of the month there were a few brief snow flurries. Aunt Hetty recovered slowly. Mrs. Ellis stayed with her, after relieving Rose. Judith managed to stop in for a moment every day. And Bill remained on the case.

Aunt Hetty's face was twisted, slightly,

but she could talk. She seemed to be glad when Judith came, with a book or some fruit or a handful of flowers. She said, once, when she was well enough for conversation, "I guess I owe you a lot."

"Not me, I just happened to find you. It's Bill you should thank."

"He's a fair doctor," said the old woman grudgingly.

That much she granted him. She submitted to all his treatments, obeyed his orders. She called him formally "Doctor" and ignored him when he spoke to her as Aunt Hetty. When he suggested that he turn her over to the Valleytown doctor she demurred. "You're good enough to take care of me, ain't you?" she said.

Her paralysis cleared up slowly and by the middle of November she was able to be up and about and dismiss Mrs. Ellis. "I can look after myself," she said.

Judith was very much alarmed at this proceeding. She argued with her, one cold dark afternoon.

"But you mustn't be alone."

"Can't afford to be waited on," said the old woman shortly: "He — he must think I'm made of money."

"Bill has paid Mrs. Ellis out of his own pocket," said Judith indignantly, "and he can't afford it either. But he's willing to. You're his patient — and his own flesh and blood. You aren't very fair to him!"

"Seems like you take up for him pretty quick," commented Aunt Hetty. She looked at Judith shrewdly and an unwilling smile tugged at the corner of her twisted mouth, "In love with him, ain't you?"

"Yes," said Judith hotly, not caring, "I am."

"Going to marry him?" persisted Aunt Hetty.

"He hasn't asked me," said Judith shortly, "and if he did I wouldn't."

"Hasn't asked you? Bigger fool than I took him for," mused Aunt Hetty, "what's the matter with him?"

Judith, her anger passed, was ashamed of herself and sorry that she had spoken. She said, "I wish you'd forget I said that. Bill doesn't think of me in that way. Besides, I told you long ago that he couldn't afford a poor wife . . . so it's just as well."

"I'll have to talk to that young man," said his aunt. "Reach me my shawl, will you, Judy?"

"You wouldn't! Oh, *please*," implored Judith, "please don't say anything about me to him."

"Who said I'd say anything? I ain't one

to meddle, Judy Gillmore. No. I been thinking about what you said about my being alone. That worthless boy Mat looks after the fire and," said Miss Hetty reluctantly, "people have been nice enough about bringing in things . . . got more in my icebox most days than I know what to do with, let alone cakes and pies in the breadbox. But I've been thinking." She would say no more.

That evening as Judith was leaving the hotel lounge to go to her room Bill came in the front door and hurried across to stop her. His face was alight, she had never seen him look so young and eager. He cried, "What do you think has happened?"

"I haven't the least idea. Here, let's sit down by the fire."

"Aunt Hetty's had a change of heart. Oh, she won't admit it. But she had a long talk with me when I stopped in just now. Says that maybe she made a mistake in planning to go on living alone. Wanted to know if I'd come live with her. Says if I can arrange to keep my office at the hotel and take my meals there I can have a room. She says she'd like to have a man around the house nights!"

"But, Bill," said Judith, "won't that

cramp your style?"

"I'll see that it doesn't. It's a sort of wedge. There are two big upstairs bedrooms she doesn't use and I could use one for a sort of study. And another thing, Judith. She said something about her other house — the one on Parker Street. Do you know it? It's quite a place. She rents it to the Hamlins now and their lease is up, first of the year. She said something about . . . if I wanted to move in there — and use downstairs for an office . . . sometime. She was pretty vague. Said rather grimly, 'We'll see how we get along.' Gosh, Judith, the Parker Street house is just right . . . and there's lots of room as well as ground. I could have an office downstairs. Aunt Hetty could have her own apartment, I'd get a woman for the cooking. It would work out fine, if this trial trip does."

"It would be wonderful," said Judith sincerely. "I'm awfully happy for you."

"It would be all due to you," he said. "She thinks the world of you, Judith, even if she doesn't show it."

A bellboy came across the lounge, "New York calling you, Miss Gillmore," he said, and Judith rose, with an apology. Bill looked after her, his brows drawn. That would be Wallace, of course. He called her almost every night, everyone in the hotel knew that by now. He came up each weekend, by plane since the weather was not as yet too stormy to fly. Sometimes he came alone, sometimes he brought people. And when he came he expected Judith to be at his disposal.

Bill rose and went back to his rooms. Much of the flavor had gone from his good news, it didn't seen to amount to much now. What did it mean anyway? Just that a grouchy old woman had decided to reconcile herself with her brother's son, and offered him a room in her cottage and a trial at being together. The Parker Street house didn't seem as big or as exciting. It would take a lot of doing over and Aunt Hetty wouldn't be too easy to get along with, he thought gloomily. Anyway, why should Judith care?

Betty stopped him in the corridor, with a long story about a sprained wrist. He took her into his office and examined it. She had wrenched it a little, falling on the ice, trying out her skates after their first really good freeze, and it was slightly swollen. He attended to it and because he was lonely and a little let down, told her about his new plans.

"Oh, Bill, then you won't live here any

more," she cried, her little face sober.

"I'll have my office here," he said. "Of course I'll have to talk to your dad."

"But if you get along — Oh, I know it's wonderful for her," said Betty, "but she's so old and cranky. I stopped to speak to her once and she barked at me. And if you go clear away and live with her in that big old house, you'll go crazy and we'll never see you."

"There'll still be stomach-aches and sprains," he reminded her, "at River-mount."

"But I shall hate your going," she said, her mutinous face close to his.

It was really an effort not to kiss her. She was a very kissable infant. Bill rose from his desk. "You run along," he said comfortably. "I'll take a look at the wrist to-morrow. And don't be downhearted. Aunt Hetty may change her mind."

"I hope she does," said Betty, and thought, I wish she'd broken her scrawny neck that time. No, I don't. But it's all so stupid, Bill going away and everything, and Judith and the old woman thick as thieves.

She left the office pondering on the in-justice in this world. There was Bert Wallace crazy about Judith and she wouldn't have him. And of course Bill was crazy about her too. As for Saks, Betty had a letter every day begging her forgiveness, begging a word. Sometimes she smiled over them. But she never answered them. She couldn't bear to think of Saks . . . not yet. And Roger Higgins, always writing her from Harvard. She answered his letters. That was fun. But she didn't take Roger seriously.

Marge's grandmother would be an invalid for the rest of her life, but she had recovered sufficiently to permit the Higgins' to go on with their plans. Marge would make her debut during the Christmas holidays and Betty would go down and stay with them. And in May they would sail for England. Her father had promised her that. But . . . she wasn't sure that she wanted to sail . . . not quite.

CHAPTER XVIII

Bert Wallace brought a party up with him by train to spend the Thanksgiving holidays, arriving the day before. He had Candace Howland, and a young, attractive married couple. Joan and Frank Norton, and his guests professed themselves enchanted with the place, and its unusually festive air. There were numerous other parties up for the short vacation, and as the weather remained cold for so long a period the river and nearby lakes were frozen solid and the skating promised to hold. There had been several recent snow flurries and the ground was white. As yet there was not enough snow for skiing, but Wednesday evening it began to descend in earnest, large unhurrying flakes and then a finer, thicker snow with a strong wind rising.

It snowed hard all night, all Thursday and all Friday. The young people dressed themselves warmly against the weather and went out in it and came back laughing and wet, their cheeks rosy. They had all been warned not to go far from the hotel as the weather-minded among the Hillhigh oldsters prophesied a regular old-fashioned blizzard. And they were right. But on Saturday it began to clear, and the even heavy grayness of the sky was flecked with blue and the sun appeared, at first a pale yellow roundness at which one could look without blenching. But finally all the clouds were gone and it was clear and still and cold, with a great shining sun and the tree branches bowed down under their weight of soft cold ermine. Perfect skiing weather everybody said and ran for their skis.

Sam, the head porter, shook his head. He had been born in Hillhigh sixty years ago. He said dolefully to Judith, "It don't look any too settled to me."

But she laughed at him, as a weather prophet he was Old Man Gloom, she said. She was too busy to worry over Sam's warning. She had entertainments to plan and, now that it had cleared, the skiers to watch over. She felt like a mother hen, a little distracted, with a large family of restless chicks. After all, most of the guests in the hotel had been cooped up since Wednesday evening and they were rarin' to go. There were, however, less adventurous souls who asked to borrow one of the many bright sleds kept in the storeroom, upon which they could whoop their way down safe little nearby hills. Others wanted their skates sharpened or demanded to know where, if any place, they could hire cutters and horses. Bill took to a sleigh for his calls. The snow was deep and it had drifted and cars were stalled all over the roads. He had already moved to Aunt Hetty's, with Mr. Corbin's approval, but came up every day for his office hours and he had a telephone installed in the Martin House, much to Aunt Hetty's horror. She admitted that he'd need one but "drat the things," she said, "just a nuisance! Ringing all hours of the night!"

Betty was occupied enough. The house was full of pleasant boys and their parents, spending the holidays . . . boys who came from nearby boarding schools and whose people met them, as it were, half way, to be with them.

"Come sleighing with us?" Bert asked Judith. But she shook her head. "I can't," she told him, "I'm busier than the proverbial one-armed paperhanger."

His glance fell on Betty. "How about you?" he inquired, smiling at her, and Betty said instantly, "I'd love to." She went off with his party a little later in an old-fashioned sleigh with the seats on the side and straw and hot bricks for their feet in the middle. Judith felt a little dubious about her going but could say nothing. Betty had been very shy with Wallace the first time she had seen him after her abortive attempt at elopement. But he soon put her at her ease and they had become the best of friends, apparently. This worried Judith, "for no good reason," she told herself. But it was obvious that Bert had found the youngster more interesting since the Boston episode. Before that he had looked on her as a pretty kid, but a very unsophisticated one, young even for her eighteen years. He was accustomed to eighteen-year-old girls who knew most of the answers and did very much as they pleased. But Betty's upbringing, at school and at Hillhigh, had been rather different. It had kept her young. And Bert was not especially drawn to genuine naïveté. But now —

Candace, Judith observed, was going to work on Bert for all she was worth — even if that wasn't very much. She usurped him, and made it quite plain to Judith that she had been seeing him frequently in town. And that the nice young Nortons were along as chaperons. The Nortons, very much in love and engaged in pursuing amusement, did not take their chaperoning seriously and Alice Norton, thought Judith, must be considerably younger than Candace.

On Sunday, Bert drew her aside.

"You have to have a moment for me, Judy. I never see you. Haven't changed your mind, have you?"

He asked her that every time he saw her and over the long-distance telephone as well. He'd even written to ask her — a departure, for Bert didn't believe in putting things on paper. But her answer today was the same as it had been on every previous occasion.

"No, Bert. Sorry."

"You aren't sorry, really!"

"Perhaps not," she admitted, smiling.

"Look, the Nortons are pulling out tonight. I'm staying on for a couple of days . . . swell weather and all."

"How about Candace?"

He shrugged. "She's returning with the Nortons," he answered, without much expression, but Judith deduced, with an inward chuckle, that he had had considerable struggle in making up her mind for her.

"Well?"

"You make it difficult for a fellow to ask you the simplest question," he grumbled. "It's this way. Monday's your day off. And

I want you to go skiing with me. How are you on skis?"

"Not so bad," she said, "I used to spend vacations up here, and moreover at school —"

But he wasn't listening.

"Then we'll go off, to Halfway House. It's a stiff climb but worth it, as I learned today . . . take along some things to cook, leave 'em there, have a picnic later."

"That would be fun," she said instantly, "we'll round up Betty and some of the others."

"I didn't include Betty."

"Wouldn't it be nicer?" she inquired. "Look, Bert, I've simply got to go now." She hurried off rather like the White Rabbit, muttering to herself, I wish I could get hold of that ski instructor.

For it looked like a busy season. The instructor wasn't due at Rivermount till the first of the month. They could have used him before that. Now he was on his way from the West and couldn't be hurried.

During that afternoon before traintime Candace developed a cold and a headache. She sneezed, looked wan and worried. "I can't," she told Bert, "I just can't travel back tonight. I'd catch more cold in the train."

Bert was not impressed but there was nothing he could do about it, and so the Nortons went off to the station by sleigh, waving a gay good-bye and Candace remained, spiking tomorrow's guns. Because, of course, that was why she had stayed, Judith decided, going to her room to inquire if there was anything she could do.

She found Candace fetching in an angora bed jacket and looking becomingly pale.

"Don't come near me. You might catch it," Candace warned her. "I wonder if you'd ask that nice Dr. Martin . . . I'm afraid I have a little temperature," she added, "and I've been scared to death of the simplest cold ever since I had pneumonia. Caught it sleigh-riding, I've no doubt," she added.

Judith said, "Of course you must take care of it," and picked up the telephone. Bill, she knew, would be at Aunt Hetty's about this time.

"Bill? Judith. Can you come up . . . or are you planning to come anyway? Miss Howland has a rather severe cold. Yes. Yes, she says so. Thanks."

She said good-bye and hung up. "He'll be right along," she said; "sure there isn't anything I can do?"

"No, I've some books . . . if you'd order some grapefruit juice for me. Oh, yes, if you see Bert around, perhaps —"

Smiling, Judith went in search of Bert. She found him standing by the big hearth in the lounge talking to Betty in markedly intimate tones. It struck her that they moved apart rather hastily when she spoke to them. She delivered Candace's message and went on to her own room.

Before dinner she encountered Bill.

"I'm eating early," he announced, "may I sit at your table?"

"Of course," she told him, "delighted."

"Hate to deprive you of Wallace's company," he said, "but he won't be down to dinner tonight."

"What do you mean, deprive?"

"Well, you've been eating with him and his party every night since they came."

"Once. Don't be silly. Is he ill too?"

"No, but Miss Howland doesn't feel well enough to brave the draft enroute to the dining room," he replied gravely, "and as a matter of fact I advised against it. I pointed out that Mr. Wallace had a pleasant sitting room adjoining her bedroom and that dinner might be served them both in there. All perfectly proper and all that sort of thing and not dangerous as the temperature of the rooms is the same."

"Playing Cupid?" she demanded.

"If I were would you be very sore?" he asked.

"Terribly," said Judith with a sober face. "I'd rush right in and 'mow 'em down,'" she added in excellent imitation of Charlie McCarthy.

Bill laughed and Judith asked:

"Is she — Candace — very ill?"

"She might be," he said cautiously.

"Bill, look me in the eye. Temperature?"

"None at all."

"Pulse?"

"Fast when I hold her hand," he said modestly.

Judith laughed. "Admit it, she hasn't a sign of a cold."

"I admit nothing. And she may have one coming on. Who knows?"

Betty was dining with some of the younger fry and Mr. Corbin was late in coming to the table, so Bill and Judith were alone for the meal. They talked about Aunt Hetty.

"How are you getting on?"

"It's an armed neutrality," he said.

"Nothing more about the Parker Street house?"

"Not yet. But I have hopes. She said, last

night, that as long as I was around I might as well stay to supper. Sets a darned good table too."

"I bet she doesn't eat much when she's alone," said Judith, "poor old thing."

"Judith . . ." But the waitress came along smiling, to say she couldn't read Bill's writing on the order slip he had filled in for both of them. When that was over, Judith asked "Well?"

"Well what?"

"You were going to say something."

"I've forgotten." Darn that waitress anyway, he thought. But it was just as well. He couldn't build on Aunt Hetty. She might throw him out tomorrow. Still he had dreamed — if he went to live in the Parker Street house. And Judith didn't mind Aunt Hetty. And she wasn't, he was beginning to believe, really interested in Wallace and all his money. If . . . if — But then along came May to inquire if he had written squash or succotash and he'd lost his nerve.

"Too bad," said Judith, "it couldn't have been very important."

"It wasn't to you. Or to me either," he said hastily. "Look, let's pretend we each have ten million dollars. What would you do with yours?"

"Fun," said Judith excitedly. "I'd settle a

million on Mother and Aunt Emily right away. And we'd have a place somewhere, here in the summer and New York, I think, winters, all together. And I'd endow some hospital for crippled children and I'd . . ."

"You haven't asked for anything for yourself," he reminded her.

"Would you let me set you up in an elegant practice? Oh, I forgot, you have ten millions of your own. Well, then, what do I like? Do you suppose I could engage Edgar Bergen to bring Charlie McCarthy over Wednesday evenings, and that I could have Wayne King and his orchestra play me to sleep, and maybe Lombardo when I want to dance? And I'd have all the jigsaw puzzles in the world, made especially. And a car. And a — no, I wouldn't want a personal maid again, too much responsibility. But on the days Charlie McCarthy couldn't come I'd ask Burns and Allen over. For tea."

"Sounds like a large order," said Bill.

"And I'd have a projection room and get all the good films. I do love the movies, Bill."

"You don't get to see many any more."

"Oh, that's all right," she said, "I don't miss them much. And I'd have all the newest novels and biographies and when we were in New York I'd go to all the first nights."

"And night clubs?"

"No, they bore me."

"Well, then," said Bill, drawing a deep breath, "as a matter of fact you wouldn't have to have ten millions for all that. I mean for your personal wants. All you'd need would be a radio . . . and of course theater tickets and seats at the movies. And a lending library. They rent puzzles too."

"That's right," she said, "that's all I'd need. And I could even go without the first nights. What about you?"

"If I had ten millions," he began, and then looked up as someone spoke his name.

"Well, Dick?"

"It's a call, Dr. Martin. You're to go to the Agnew house on South Street right away."

"Hell and damn!" said Bill rising. "There goes my ten millions. As well as my desert. The Agnew baby has decided to arrive ahead of time."

She watched him leave. She thought, I wonder what he was going to say.

But if it had been — that. It couldn't be. You didn't need ten millions to tell a girl you loved her. If you did love her.

CHAPTER XIX

Monday was sunny, clear and cold. There were heavy clouds low over the mountains and Sam was the only one who believed that they portended more snow. But people were so accustomed to Sam's prognostications that no one paid much attention. The weather report promised fair clear weather, ideal for winter sports, Bert told Judith.

Judith was curious to learn what Candace would be up to, now that she had won her point and was staying on. She did not appear for breakfast and when, at the time Bert had designated, Judith arrived in the lounge equipped with warm garments and a pair of skis which the game room had furnished her, she found Bert alone and ready, with a professional-looking pack in which he assured her was the makings of lunch. He had planned to reach their objective about noon, cook lunch and then do their spot of skiing.

"Where's Betty?" asked Judith. "I spoke to her last night and she said she'd be delighted to join us — Tommy Dean is staying over and she was going to ask him."

"I just saw her," said Bert, "there'll be some delay. I suggested we go out, and they'll join us. Tommy had to wait for a long-distance from his father and Betty would wait for him."

"What about Candace?" asked Judith. "She'll hate to miss the party, although she doesn't care much for winter sports."

Bert's face was grave. "Poor child," he murmured, "she thinks she is well enough to join us. But I persuaded her that it would be very foolish. I left her snug in bed, with a pitcher of fruit juice beside her and an armful of the latest magazines and novels from the newsstand."

Judith concealed a smile. She had a vivid mental picture of Candace arguing that her cold had evaporated, as it were, and Bert explaining soberly that it would be the height of folly to rise from a bed of pain — or at least sniffles — and venture into the cold wet snow. There was nothing Candace could do about that, short of admitting that she hadn't had the vestige of a cold.

Bert had a sleigh and driver waiting and they drove to the foot of the trail leading up to Halfway House, the guest cabin maintained by the hotel for summer outings and winter sports. Bert told the driver when to return and they got out and started up the trail.

"It may not be sporting," said Judith firmly, "but I am not going to climb this on skis. I'm going up on my two well-shod feet. It's a lot quicker and, so far as I'm concerned, safer."

It was hard going, they slipped and slithered and once Judith slid into the deep-piled snow on the side of the trail. Bert pulled her out, brushed her off, and they went on, using their ski poles as support. Once he called back, "You look very fetching in blue gabardine and a red toque," but that was the extent of their personal conversation.

The log cabin seemed almost luxurious . . . there was a great fire ready to be kindled, and plenty of logs, paper and kindlings. In a short time Bert had the fire going and the deathlike chill of the place dispelled. Cutlery and paper plates and tin cups were at hand, there would be plenty of hot water after Bert got the kerosene stove going. The rough table even had a red cloth and there were big fur rugs, and comfortable rustic chairs.

Judith struggled out of an extra sweater, mittens and scarf and watched Bert light the kerosene stove. "Be careful, don't blow us up," she warned, and then "Wouldn't it have been awful if you'd forgotten to bring the keys and we had to go back again, lunchless?"

"But an elephant never forgets," he reminded her.

She went to the door and looked down the mountain and then up the trail to the first ski jump. It was fairly stiff, she thought, but she could manage it if she didn't attempt any fancy work. The sunlight was cold and clear, and long blue shadows lay on the snow . . . you could see the world, or a lot of it, from halfway up the mountain. You felt small and lost but exhilarated.

"Get busy," ordered Bert, "I'm starved." He came up to smack her on the shoulder, comradewise, and Judith turned and went back into the cookstove alcove.

The hotel had provided steaks, potatoes cut for frying, a can of shortening for frying, a bottle of cream, coffee, fruit and cake, and water. "I swing a mean steak," said Judith, but halted. "I wonder," she added, "if I should wait till we see the kids coming along the trail."

"They aren't coming," Bert announced calmly.

"Bert!" She stared at him angrily. Then

she sighed. "I might have known," she murmured. "I'm a fool, it was perfectly obvious from the first. But what on earth did you tell Betty?"

"I had a little chat with her last night," he said, unashamed. "I asked her — as a favor, you understand — to accept the invitation ostensibly and then to forget to come."

"She's under obligations to you," said Judith slowly, "and has been so frightened, poor kid, that you'll tell somebody about the Boston business. You mentioned that, no doubt," she added, "didn't you? A touch of blackmail!"

"Not exactly," he said, undisturbed, "I just said 'fair exchange is no robbery' or something like that. She was perfectly willing; in fact, she thinks it's all good clean fun."

"Are you sure she thinks that?" inquired Judith, with a frying pan in one hand.

Bert dodged, in a pretense of fear.

"Don't hit me, lady, I'll come down," he paraphrased. "I don't know what she thinks. If she thinks I wanted to be alone with you, why, that's all right with me, as it happens to be the truth."

"Listen," said Judith, "why all this elaborate intrigue? It doesn't make sense."

"Would you have come with me alone?" he asked.

"No," she said after a moment, "yes . . . I don't know. But I admit that when I suggested Betty and Tom and you agreed I was much more willing."

"There you are," he said triumphantly. "I haven't any evil designs on you, my dear, unless wanting to marry you comes under that category. I'm really not much of a menace."

"Yes, you are," said Judith slowly, "you're more of a menace since you stopped being smart-aleck and show-off and began to be rather nice than you were before, I think."

He took a step toward her. "Then you mean —" he began eagerly, but she waved him back with the pan.

"No, I don't mean that," she said firmly. "I mean you're more of a menace because I suspect it's an act. Front. Façade. Whatever you want to call it. A man doesn't alter what appears to be his basic character as quickly as you seemed to, Bert, despite what the books tell us about the ennobling influence of a great love. Because I don't believe in your great love. I've known you too long and too well. I think you're a spoiled boy who can't get what he wants

279

one way so he tries another."

He tried to smile and succeeded, but his eyes were not pleasant. Judith caught her breath and turned back to the stove. For the first time in her knowledge of him she was really frightened.

But all he said, cheerfully enough, was:

"Okay by me, baby, if that's the way you feel. Not that you're right. You couldn't be more wrong. How about a little lunch . . . ?"

She said, "I oughtn't. I ought to go back."

"It's a long walk from the foot of the mountain to Rivermount. Our equipage has orders to call for us, later. You wouldn't sit in a snowbank all that time, would you? It would be pretty silly. Besides, villains don't come swooping on skis. It is a sport that isn't conducive to romance, not while you're indulging in it anyway."

She said, "All right, you win. But I don't feel especially flattered and I don't think any the better of you for it."

She had made up her mind that she would say no more than that. They'd have their lunch and their skiing and then they would go down the trail again and meet the sleigh. And that would be that. And after this experience, job or no job, and yes, even Betty or no Betty, she would avoid Mr. Bert Wallace as much as possible. For she had no doubt that he would hold Betty over her head. He was capable of it. She should never have asked for his help that night. She could have traced the child by herself. But she had no idea, when she started out, that she would find her so soon, and nearby. She had thought she might have to run over half a dozen states before she found her. She had been frightened and so had turned to Bert.

But she wouldn't, ever again.

Lunch was good, the steaks and potatoes perfection, the coffee superb, the cake and fruit all that one could expect. Bert, passing his cup, remarked, "You are one of the world's wonders, a woman who can really make good coffee."

"It's the measuring and timing," she said solemnly, "likewise the old-fashioned pot. I love them. And the good spring water. Why don't they keep it up here?"

"It will freeze, silly."

"So will we if we sit around a fire and then go out into the snow. I feel more reluctant every moment. Let's wash up and get going," she suggested, gathering the cutlery and cups together. "You do the pans. I hate to!"

Presently they had shut and locked the cabin, after kicking out what remained of the fire, and were off again up the trail to the first ski jump. It took some time. But when they finally reached it and looked out over the wide wonder of New England in winter, Judith caught her breath. It was more beautiful than she had remembered.

For the next hour or so she was too intent on keeping her balance to think. Not that she always kept it. Once Bert pulled her out of a snowbank into which she had landed head first. And several times he had to help her up. He was a fine skier, almost professionally good.

Better than the ski jump Judith liked skiing across the long valley of snow. It wasn't as exhilarating but it was much less alarming.

After what seemed like a long time, she said:

"I haven't the remotest idea of the time, Bert, but hadn't we better start back? It's growing a little dark, even."

"Just clouds. Look, let's try the high jump. That one is only for beginners."

"Not me," she said firmly. "I've decided I'm a beginner too. But I'll come up with you and watch you do your stuff."

But before they reached the farther,

highest jump, it had started to snow and the sky was uniformly overcast.

"We've got to get back," said Judith anxiously.

"Nonsense, it's just a flurry. Oh, all right, if you're so worried, but — One jump then, come on, be a sport. How about it? I've been fooling around with that baby jump just to keep you company. That's not for a man."

"Very well," she said. But she was still anxious. However, it was not snowing very hard and perhaps he was right, it was a flurry and would pass.

She stood on the top of the high jump and watched him take off. That's what it reminded her of, a plane, a bird in flight. Everything was beautifully timed. But suddenly, disaster . . . he wavered, did not recover himself, and fell, sprawling and skidding.

She cupped her hands about her mouth and shouted, "I told you so!" But he did not stir. There was no answering hail. He did not get to his feet again.

She said, aloud, "He's hurt . . . perhaps badly."

She looked at the jump. She was not sufficiently expert, she realized, to make it except by luck and it seemed to her that it was snowing harder now.

She took off her skis, slung them across her back and started off stumbling and slipping in her heavy boots down the trail. It took so long to reach him and the snow was blowing from every direction. The sky was darker now, a wind had risen. It cut her cheeks, and tears were on her lashes and froze there. She was cold and frightened. It was so far down the trail to where the sleigh would be waiting soon.

When she reached him he was struggling to rise, on one elbow.

"Bert —"

"I've broken my leg, damn it!" he said, and despite the increasing cold, sweat ran down his face. "You've got to do something . . . get me to the cabin . . . somehow . . . get my skis off," he ordered, watching her as, fumbling a little, she obeyed.

His right leg was useless. Judith looked at the skis and thought of splints. But she didn't know much about splinting, she might do more harm than good. The cabin was situated below them . . . not very far. She thought and then spoke. "I'll do what I can," she said, "you'll just have to stand it."

"My God," he said, "I'll freeze to death . . . this storm and all."

I'll freeze to death!

She took off her heavy scarf and despite his protestations, which were almost screams, bandaged his leg as best she could.

She took her skis and lashed them to his. She had an extra scarf, he had one, there were the leather thongs. She fashioned, after what seemed an eternity, a fairly creditable sled. And somehow pushed him along the flat stretch of open plain which was the end of the jump and then down the incline to the trail past the cabin. She had to guide the sled and to hold it back when it threatened to run away from her, spill him out and do more damage. Once she believed that he had fainted, he was still for so long.

It seemed years before they reached the trail and comparative safety. Bert said, speaking for the first time, "I might crawl."

He couldn't stand, that much was evident. Painfully he crawled as far as the door and fainted again. Beating her mittened hands together, the increasingly heavy snow blinding her, she managed somehow after awkward failures to get the key of the cabin out of his pocket, drag his heavy weight across the threshold and close the door.

Then, after helping him to inch across the floor, she put a pillow from a chair under his head, and one of the fur rugs over him although the added weight made him curse with pain.

Sobbing under her breath Judith relaid the fire and lit it . . . it smoked, she kicked back the logs. She lit the stove, and measured coffee into the pot. If only she had some brandy.

Bert spoke heavily:

"If we aren't there waiting for the sleigh, he'll go away."

"Of course he won't," she said, turning, "he'll wait. When we don't come he'll know something's wrong . . . and get help. We have warmth and food, it's just a question of being patient."

"You'd talk about patience," he said, "if your leg was broken! No, he won't wait, I told him not to."

"You told him —"

"Well?" he demanded.

She set the pot on the stove. Her hands were shaking and she felt sick, but her voice was steady.

"Why?" she inquired.

"Don't be a damned fool," he said, irritated. "I thought, well, if we're here overnight . . . the last weather report said storm."

"You lied to me."

"Don't be melodramatic. Sure I lied. We had plenty of food, I saw to that . . . and firewood. I wanted time to persuade you and a situation which might add persuasion. Don't look like that!"

"But the hotel — the people —" she said slowly.

"Do you suppose I'd care what they thought? Besides, if it did storm, my excuse was perfect. No one can guard against accidents of nature."

She said, "So I was to spend the night here with you whether I wanted to or not."

He said, "I didn't break my leg on purpose. I wouldn't love any woman enough for that."

CHAPTER XX

After a moment Judith said, "I could go down the trail, and wait till someone passes, if the sleigh isn't there."

"It won't be. And you can't leave me alone," he said, his voice rising. "The fire might go out. Or something might catch and I'd burn to death — helpless —"

"If we don't come back they'll send someone from the hotel. The driver will report."

"I told the driver if we didn't show up in fifteen minutes we might have come down earlier and picked up the early Valleytown bus . . . the highway runs across the mountain road which leads to the trail. It has been cleared."

"You think of everything," she said bitterly.

The storm was increasing in velocity. The windows rattled and they heard the soft slurring of the snow. There was a cold draft from the chimney.

She had done what she could to make him comfortable. She sat thinking. Then, "They will send from the hotel when we don't come back. Betty will . . . and," she added after a moment, "Bill Martin."

"In this storm tonight? They'll wait till morning."

"No," said Judith, "Bill won't."

"You're pretty sure of him, aren't you?"

"Yes, I am. Of his friendship and his loyalty. That's all one needs to be sure of, Bert."

"Well, I can't stay here all night," he said.

"I offered to go — but you were afraid to be left alone," she reminded him.

He said uneasily, "If it gets colder —"

"I'd fix the fire . . . and nothing will happen, there's a big spark screen," she said.

"The chimney might catch."

"Oh, Bert," she said despairingly, "what do you want me to do?"

There was a long silence. He said harshly, "I've got to have medical attention . . . I'll take the chance."

Judith got to her feet. She pulled on her wet mittens. She had now no scarf except the lighter one. But that, and Bert's, had lashed the skis together, they were outside, wet. She buttoned her collar high after putting on the extra sweater she had removed after they came in. She thought aloud:

"There's no house nearby on the mountain road . . . but I can get to the highway, walking, if no one comes by. There are houses there, and telephones."

"You'll hurry?" he asked.

The cabin was warmth, light, shelter. Outside the snow was driving in swirling, biting flakes. If she lost her way, if she lost the trail, now hidden from her, if she stumbled and fell and died there on the mountainside? She hesitated, her hand on the door and looked back at the fire, on which she had recently put the two big logs. She had hurt her back and strained her arms but she had managed. They would burn a long time, as long as it would take her to get to the bottom of the mountain and safety. If she got there. The fire looked safe, the cabin looked safe . . . but Bert spoke impatiently. "Well," he said, "get going, can't you?"

Outside, the door closed between her and warmth, between her and security, Judith began to laugh silently. Love, she thought, is a wonderful thing! A man makes elaborate plans, she went on thinking, struggling to orient herself — here was the trail . . . if only she could keep on it — to force her to stay with him in a mountainside cabin overnight. Why? Because he loved her! But before that he breaks his leg, which wasn't part of his plan, and he is therefore in pain. Where's love then? Self-preservation, she thought crazily, slipping, falling, getting to her feet, is the first law. Bert obeyed it. Why didn't I? Why didn't I stay in the cabin, no matter what he said or did? He couldn't do much, he's hardly in his present condition a physical menace!

She was trying not to sob, her lungs hurt her, the snow blinded her, and the sky was very dark. There was just a faint gray light by which she fought her way along the trail. Sometimes she missed it. Often she fell and lay there gasping. Then she struggled painfully to her feet and went on, always finding the trail again by some miracle. The tears the wind exacted were again frozen on her lashes, she was cold clear through, she ached in every bone in her body.

The last time she fell she thought she would never get up. She was so terribly tired. She felt, even, a little drowsy. She must, she thought, be losing her mind. She heard voices. People always heard voices when they lost their minds.

She got to her hands and knees, wavered to her feet. The snow had not ceased, it was thicker than ever. How much farther

. . . how much farther?

The voices did not stop, they sounded louder and nearer. They must be real voices. She tried to call out and found that she could not. She made a strangled sound . . . and Bill heard her.

"Judith — *Judith* — !"

That was a real voice, Bill's voice. Or was she going crazy again? She began to run in sliding, stumbling steps. "Bill," she called and her voice came back to her. "Bill!"

He bulked before her, looming up among the shadows. His arms were around her. "Steady," he said quietly, "where's Wallace?"

"At the cabin," she gasped, not believing the security, the utter relief that flooded her, "his leg is broken."

Still holding her, Bill issued his short commands to the men he had brought with him. He and Sam would go on up to the cabin. Dick was to take Miss Gillmore down the rest of the way and get her to the hotel. Mark — and now Judith recognized the faces about her, the last one of the guide who took out skiing parties — Mark would go back and commandeer a sled. A stretcher was out of the question on the trail in a storm. He would stay with

Wallace till they got back. They were to bring one of the big sleighs.

Judith said, low, "I thought you wouldn't come, I hoped you would."

She felt his mittened hand on her numb cheek. He said, "I came . . . you should have known."

She had, it appeared, almost reached the end of the trail, and with Dick's strong arm around her she stumbled the rest of the way and to a waiting sleigh. They didn't talk. They saved their breath and reached the road and the driver whipped up his horses and they were headed toward the Rivermount.

It was Betty who met her, took her in charge and got her to bed, between warm blankets and hot-water bottles. Bill had left orders before he left. And Betty sat beside her while she sobbed and shivered into something approaching quiet.

"It was my fault," said Betty, after a time.

"No, Bert's. He told you not to come. I'm glad you didn't. Because you would have been caught there too."

"When you didn't come back," said Betty, "I called Roberts at the livery. He told me what Bert Wallace had told him. It sounded — crazy to me. So I told Bill when he came in and meantime it had begun to storm."

After a time of just lying there, safe in warmth and comfort, Judith asked:

"Roberts had been to the foot of the trail?"

"Yes, at four, as Bert said. He waited fifteen minutes. Then he came back."

"Thank heaven you told Bill," said Judith, "I'm so grateful — Betty. I suppose I would have made the trail. But it was hard going. I could have stayed in the cabin but Bert didn't want me to, except just at first . . . when he was afraid of being left alone."

"Bill," reported Betty, "was like a crazy man." She swallowed. It was the hardest thing she had ever said. But not so hard as something she must say. "He's so terribly in love with you," she added.

"Oh, no," said Judith, "no."

"Yes, he is. Judy, when I told Marge I had seen you in his arms, I had. . . . No, don't interrupt. It was the morning you found — you know, the man who shot himself. I was riding along the river. You had fainted, Bill had you in his arms. I heard him say 'Judith, my darling'. . ."

"But," cried Judith, sitting up against the pillow, her eyes brilliant, her cheeks flushed, "why didn't you tell me when I asked you in the train?"

"I saw that you didn't know. That you'd really been unconscious. So I didn't *want* to tell you . . . You see," said Betty, "I — I'm in love with him too."

"My dear —"

Betty lifted her chin. She said, with little girl dignity, "I'll get over it. I'm just a kid, I guess. I've been such a fool. And mean . . . about Saks too. That was all my fault. I don't feel the way I did toward him now . . . since I knew how Bill really feels about you. And you too," she asked, "you too?"

"Of course," said Judith, "how could I help it?"

"Everything's so mixed up," said Betty. "But you're safe, Judy . . . and things will come out all right. And I'll be going away soon, to Boston and then to Europe. Maybe when I come back I might even want to see Saks again," she said slowly.

She'd be in love half a dozen times before then, thought Judith. Or maybe not. But out of love, surely, with Bill. Then perhaps Saks would come back again to Rivermount, to Betty. Perhaps things would work out.

"I could kill Bert Wallace!" said Betty definitely.

"Don't bother. His broken leg is enough. He'll be laid up here," said Judith, "for a long time, unless he insists on getting himself back to town on a stretcher through a car window. I don't know. But wherever he goes or stays Candace will be with him, I imagine."

She could see that too, a little more plainly than her other attempt at clairvoyance. Candace, all nursing instinct of the more decorative sort — and Bert quite helpless. She began to laugh and Betty looked at her in alarm. "I believe you've a fever!" she said.

"No, I haven't." But she went on laughing. She couldn't tell Betty the joke. But it was one, the funniest she had ever heard. For if she knew anything about women, Candace would make hay while the sun shone. And she was willing to bet next month's salary that Bert Wallace would be married before he knew it.

Mr. Corbin, sympathetic and disturbed, came in to hear an expurgated account of the day's events. But Judith saw that she was not convincing him in the least. He understood perfectly, although he didn't say so. His only comment was "As long as you're safe, my dear, nothing else matters."

Dinner was sent her on a tray and Betty

practically fed her. "But your own dinner?" protested Judith anxiously.

"I couldn't eat a mouthful," said Betty, and then cleaned up most of the tray under Judith's amused eyes.

And after a long time, Bill.

Betty opened the door to his knock. She signaled for silence and whispered, "Judy's asleep." She yawned. "Late, isn't it? I got more hot-water bottles — and she had some supper. She says she feels all right, as I told you when you phoned a little while ago. She was asleep then too, didn't even hear the bell ring." She was a child anxious for praise.

He said, smiling at her:

"You're a great little nurse, Betty. Thanks a lot." He patted her shoulder. "Run along now, I've got Mrs. Ellis waiting for me in my office. She'll take the room next door and look after Judith. We must wait and see how this exposure is going to turn out. I talk like a photographer!"

"Mr. Wallace is very sick — I hope?" asked Betty.

Bill laughed.

"Hospital, broken leg," he reported, "fracture reduced and X-rayed. No, he's all right."

Betty closed the door softly. Her life was blighted. But now that it had happened, now that she, too, had made her confession, she felt very much better. Debuts were fun. Europe was fun. Poor Saks, she thought, walking to her room.

After a while Judith opened her eyes. Bill sat there beside her, his hand over hers.

"You came?"

"As soon as I could. I phoned Betty when I reached the hospital with Wallace. He'll be all right."

"I mean, you came — back there on the trail."

"Of course. Betty told me . . . I talked to Roberts. Wallace," said Bill, "is a fool. I'd like to break his neck. But it's his leg. I wish I'd had the pleasure."

"I thought Betty was going with us. I didn't know what he'd told Roberts," she said.

"Of course not. Don't talk. I will. I haven't ten millions, darling, but I have Aunt Hetty and the Parker Street house. She'll give it to us as a wedding present. I telephoned her, you see, I knew she'd worry when I didn't come home although she'd never admit it. And she said, 'You marry that fool girl, Bill, and keep her out of trouble, and if you do, I'll give you the

Parker Street house.' "

He paused and Judith said dreamily, "I hope she'll live with us."

"Then you do love me?"

"So much — Oh, couldn't you kiss me," she inquired, a little dolefully, "and stop talking?"

It was an effective way.

Much later, he said contentedly:

"I've loved you since I all but knocked you down last spring but —"

"You're crazy," she said. "You have everything, including Aunt Hetty and the Parker Street house. But I'm — penniless, dearest. I'll be a burden. I swore to Aunt Hetty that I wouldn't marry you even if you asked me!"

"You aren't penniless," he said firmly, "you see, she's giving the house to *you!*"

A moment later she asked:

"When are we going to be married? I always wanted to be married in the spring. Spring's so lovely in Hillhigh."

"Spring," said Bill, "is a long way off. What about tomorrow?"

"Tomorrow," she told him, "is all right. Or any day . . . any day. I love you so much, I thought I'd die loving you — ever since last May — May and December," she said slowly; slowly her eyes were closing.

She was asleep. He put her back among the pillows and sat watching her, the tossed red hair, the broad white lids hiding black eyes, the curve of her cheek, the smiling red mouth. He bent quietly and laid his own upon it and she stirred and spoke his name.

Presently he got to his feet and went to the telephone to ask the operator to ring Mrs. Ellis in his office and ask her to come to Miss Gillmore's room. Judith slept, serene and smiling as a child. He stood by the bed looking at her until Mrs. Ellis came. Tomorrow . . . or as soon as possible. She'd want to go home, he thought, or have her people here with her when they were married. And then they would be together, for all the tomorrows.

He thought of her lashing the skis together, dragging Bert Wallace to the cabin, leaving him there and struggling out into the storm. For a man she despised . . . she didn't have to assure him that she despised Wallace. If she would do that for a man she despised, what would she not do for the man she loved?

He was that man.

We hope you have enjoyed this Large Print book. Other Thorndike Press or Chivers Press Large Print books are available at your library or directly from the publishers.

For more information about current and up-coming titles, please call or write, without obligation, to:

Publisher
Thorndike Press
295 Kennedy Memorial Drive
Waterville, ME   04901
Tel. (800) 223-1244

OR

Chivers Press Limited
Windsor Bridge Road
Bath BA2 3AX
England
Tel. (0225) 335336

All our Large Print titles are designed for easy reading, and all our books are made to last.

S4 Sta
F1 Bir
C2 Ham
R2 How
F4 Kit
S3 Coc.
R3 Gri
S1 Stra.
C2 Sim
F4 Dug.
M1 Vio